Quarantine at Alexander Abraham's

Storybook written by
Fiona McHugh

Based on the Sullivan Films Production
written by Heather Conkie
adapted from the novels of

Lucy Maud Montgomery

HarperCollins*Publishers*Ltd

QUARANTINE AT ALEXANDER ABRAHAM'S
Storybook written by Fiona McHugh

Copyright © 1991 by HarperCollins Publishers Ltd,
Sullivan Films, Inc., Ruth Macdonald and David Macdonald

Based on the Sullivan Films Production produced by Sullivan Films Inc.
in association with CBC and the Disney Channel with the participation of
Telefilm Canada adapted from Lucy Maud Montgomery's novels.

Teleplay written by Heather Conkie
Copyright © 1989 by Heather Conkie

Canadian Cataloguing in Publication Data
McHugh, Fiona
Quarantine at Alexander Abraham's
(Road to Avonlea; #5)
Based on the t.v. series: Road to Avonlea.
ISBN 0-00-647038-6
I. Title. II. Series.
PS8575.H84Q3 1991   jC813'.54   C91-093300-6
PZ7.M35Qu 1991

Design by Andrew Smith Graphics Inc.
91 92 93 94 95 OFF 10 9 8 7 6 5 4 3 2 1

Quarantine at Alexander Abraham's

Also available in the Road to Avonlea Series

The Journey Begins
The Story Girl Earns Her Name
Song of the Night
The Materializing of Duncan McTavish
Conversions

Next in the Series

Aunt Abigail's Beau
Malcolm and the Baby
Felicity's Challenge

Chapter One

Sara gazed longingly at the crimson silk. Amidst the din and clutter of the Avonlea general store, it shimmered softly from the counter, like an invitation to a dream. She could imagine herself wrapped in its glowing folds on her way to a ball, a creature of light and laughter. She wondered whether her Aunt Olivia might possibly share this appealing vision, and prayed that she might. But Aunt Olivia was fingering a dull, cotton print and murmuring words like "practical," "sensible" and "perfect for school." Such words did nothing for Sara's imagination.

As discreetly as she could, she edged the silken fabric towards the cotton, until it spread itself over the dim print like a river of fire, extinguishing, in Sara's eyes, all comparisons.

"It's so beautiful, isn't it Aunt Olivia?" she breathed. "Doesn't it make you think of birds of paradise and fiery sunsets?"

A frown creased Aunt Olivia's normally serene forehead. "It *is* lovely, Sara. But I don't think it's exactly what Hetty had in mind for your everyday school-wear. Besides, birds of paradise don't really belong in a one-room schoolhouse, now do they?"

Yet even as she spoke, Olivia's artistic eye could not help but admire the way the vibrant fabric caught and reflected the light. Without thinking, she lifted the bolt of silk from the counter, the better to admire it. No sooner had she done so than a harsh voice made her jump guiltily.

"Olivia King!" The voice stabbed through the crowded store, causing heads to turn. "Olivia King, I am *amazed* that you would even *consider* such material. That's silk, that is! Silk smacks of luxury and idleness. What's more, it is *red* silk! Red is certainly not an appropriate color for a young lady."

To her utmost mortification, Olivia found herself confronted by Rachel Lynde, who had been eavesdropping on her conversation with Sara.

"Oh, Mrs. Lynde," she stammered, her cheeks competing with the crimson silk. "I—I—only wanted to look at it, to admire it, you see. I wasn't really considering *buying* it. I mean..."

Sara leaned forward and caught the bolt of fabric as it slipped from Olivia's grasp. Exasperation rose within her. Why, oh *why* did Mrs. Lynde have to interfere, just when it looked as if Aunt Olivia were beginning to soften towards the silk? What did Rachel Lynde know about the poetry of colors anyway? She only ever seemed to dress in the drabbest of grays and browns. Indeed, today she was clothed entirely in sensible brown serge, which made her look, Sara thought, as if she were drowning in a mud puddle.

Regretfully, Sara replaced the silk on the counter and bade it a mental farewell.

Behind Rachel's imposing bulk, Sara could see Marilla Cuthbert hovering. It was plain from the expression on Marilla's face that she did not enjoy hovering, but it was a skill at which she was becoming adept. It enabled her to prevent Rachel, Avonlea's foremost busybody, from fanning the sparks of an argument into a flaming row.

Rachel Lynde had come to live at Green Gables after the death of her husband, Thomas, and the departure from Avonlea of Anne Shirley, the high-spirited orphan Marilla had come to love as her own child. Although Marilla welcomed Rachel's company, she sometimes resented having to act as keeper of the public peace. As a woman who valued her privacy, this was not a role she cherished. Yet she performed it with as good a grace as she could muster. Only occasionally did she allow her exasperation at Rachel's interfering ways to get the better of her.

Sara had lived in Avonlea long enough to be aware of Marilla's predicament. And so, because she liked and valued Miss Cuthbert, she refrained from telling Mrs. Lynde exactly what she thought of her. Instead she tried a more indirect route.

"Don't you like red, Mrs. Lynde?" she asked, with what she hoped was a sweet smile. "I just love it. I feel so much more clever when I'm wearing red than when I'm wearing any other color. Take brown, for instance. I don't know what it is about brown, but it makes me feel impossibly dull."

Mrs. Lynde glared at Sara. Was the child trying to make a fool out of her? But Sara's face expressed nothing but helpfulness.

"Perhaps you should try wearing red yourself, Mrs. Lynde," she suggested. "Just think, it might do wonders for your intelligence."

Rachel drew herself up to her full height. Surely the little rascal was not suggesting that she, Rachel Lynde, a pillar of the community, should stoop to scarlet?

"Me? Wear red? I'd go to the grave sooner. Red's the devil's color, child. Just you remember that."

As if to add weight to her warning, she turned to Reverend Leonard, who had stepped up to the counter to settle his bill. "Don't you agree, Reverend?"

A mild-mannered man at the best of times, Reverend Leonard made it a policy to avoid public skirmishes with the likes of Rachel Lynde. Startled to find himself addressed in such ringing tones, he dropped his change on the floor.

"I beg your pardon, Mrs. Lynde? What did you say?" he asked as he stooped and fumbled. "I didn't quite catch—"

Rachel raised her voice to an even more piercing level. "I said," she roared, "that the color red is definitely not appropriate!"

That same inappropriate color flooded the minister's face. "As a matter of fact," he mumbled,

"I've always been rather partial to red. I remember a fire engine I had as a child. A mere toy, it was..."

But Rachel was not interested in childhood memories, especially not red ones.

"It's a crying shame that only fools enter the ministry nowadays, Reverend Leonard!" She sniffed. "I must say, you set a fine example to the young people of Avonlea."

Marilla closed her eyes in despair. Whatever would Rachel say next? What if Reverend Leonard took offence, demanded an apology? But no. Opening her eyes, Marilla saw that Reverend Leonard had not collapsed under Rachel's direct assault. Instead, the hint of a smile seemed to tug at the corners of his mouth. Straightening his shoulders, he looked Mrs. Lynde in the eye.

"Why, Mrs. Lynde," he said slowly, and it seemed to Marilla that his voice contained a challenge. "I had no idea you were so concerned about Avonlea's young people. Perhaps, in that case, you would consent to take a class in Sunday school?"

A wry smile flickered across Marilla's face. "What a wonderful opportunity, Rachel," she commented. "Just think how you could...mold... all those young minds."

Rachel glared at Marilla, then at Reverend

Leonard, and then, for good measure, at Sara and Olivia. She felt just the tiniest bit befuddled. She had to admit that the idea of teaching Sunday school appealed to her, but the request had come from Reverend Leonard, and it had always been a matter of principle with Rachel never to do any-thing a man asked her to do—especially not a man with whom she had crossed verbal swords. This principle had worked for Rachel throughout most of her married life and she saw no reason to aban-don it merely because she was now a widow. Despite long years of contented married life, Rachel remained deeply suspicious of men. The more Rachel saw of men, the more she preferred budgies.

It was on the tip of her tongue to refuse to have anything to do with Sunday school, just to thwart Reverend Leonard, but she hesitated. Marilla was right. The thought of all those juvenile minds just waiting to be molded seemed too tempting a proposition to resist. She would *not* resist. Why should she?

Thus decided, Rachel addressed Reverend Leonard in what she considered just the right tone: a compelling mixture of condescension and sympathy.

"I can see quite plainly that the challenge of grooming young minds is proving too much for you, Reverend," she said. "I am sure you need all the help I may be able to give you. Which class would you like me to teach?"

Reverend Leonard smiled gratefully. He had not expected Mrs. Lynde to accept his challenge so readily.

"There are two classes, Mrs. Lynde, each needing a teacher. One of boys and one of girls. You may have your choice."

"Then I shall take the boys," answered Rachel decidedly. "It's true they will eventually grow up to be men, more's the pity. But since this is inevitable, one may as well try to limit the damage as much as possible." She flapped her gloves at Reverend Leonard. "Just let me loose amongst them, Reverend. I'll soon whip them into shape for you."

Reverend Leonard looked dubious. He had expected Rachel Lynde to choose the girls.

"They are a very wild set of boys, I'm afraid," he said.

"I've never known boys who weren't," retorted Rachel, firing each finger into its allotted place in her glove with military precision.

"I...I think perhaps you would like the girls better," he suggested timidly.

A vague recollection of Rachel's reputed dislike

of men had begun to surface in his memory. What if she should prove too harsh with the boys? The thought of hordes of outraged parents pounding on the manse door, grumbling about Rachel's treatment of their sons, unsettled him. But it was too late. Rachel had set her heart on molding young minds, and if they were to be male minds, then so much the better.

"Remember, Reverend, it's not what *I* like best that must be considered," she reproached him. "It is what is best for those boys. I feel that *I* shall be best for *them*."

With a gracious nod, she swept out of the store.

Marilla picked up her parcels and prepared to follow Rachel. Her eyes met those of Reverend Leonard.

"And Heaven help those poor boys!" she murmured.

A cloud of worry settled over Reverend Leonard, as the door closed behind Marilla. Had he been too impulsive, he wondered? Should he write to Mrs. Lynde and retract his offer? Taking out his handkerchief, he mopped his brow. How quickly a tiny outing to the general store had deteriorated into a nightmare!

A voice distracted him from his troubled thoughts.

"Don't worry, Reverend," said Olivia King gently. "Mrs. Lynde will manage those boys just fine. Don't you agree, Sara?"

But Sara's attention was elsewhere. Her eyes were fixed regretfully on the crimson silk, which Mr. Lawson was in the act of returning to its place on the highest shelf behind the counter.

Chapter Two

Rachel had already heaved herself onto the buggy by the time Marilla caught up with her.

"Rachel Lynde," she exploded. "Your lack of tact never ceases to amaze me!"

"I have no tact," answered Rachel. There was, Marilla thought, a certain smugness in her tone. "I am noted for that."

"Lack of tact is not something of which one should boast, Rachel."

"Tact is a tendency to saunter around to a given point, Marilla, rather than making a beeline for it. I prefer the beeline."

"Yes, and the sting, too. You had no call to treat poor Reverend Leonard in such a—a—a waspish fashion."

"Even ministers need wholesome correction

now and again, Marilla. Even they were once rowdy little boys."

For once, Marilla's sympathies were all with rowdy little boys, but she held her peace. It was not for her to point out that Rachel risked certain failure as teacher of a boys' Sunday school class.

Rachel glanced over at her friend.

"You think I shall fail, don't you? Don't worry. I do not often fail when I make up my mind to do a thing. I am noted for that, Marilla."

The day on which Rachel Lynde took over the boys' class at Sunday school was to go down in the annals of Avonlea as the day on which rowdyism was routed—horse, foot and artillery.

Into a room full of hitting, scratching and yelling boys sailed Mrs. Lynde, decked out in her drabbest of drab attire.

Marching straight to the front of the class, she paused, taking stock, as it were, of the battlefield. Pandemonium reigned. Silently, Rachel called to mind previous campaigns she had waged and won. Then she drew a long, slow breath, squared her shoulders and commenced her attack.

She did not stir from her spot. She merely gazed around her. As her eyes brought each boy, in turn, within her range of fire, she took careful aim, as though raking each one with her glance. The effect was remarkable. It seemed as if the room were being gradually sprayed with silence. Those boys on whom she had turned her gaze stiffened and slowed, their yells arrested in their throats. Even those who had not yet felt her glare quietened instinctively.

There was no mistaking it. A military might had entered the room. Rachel's weapons consisted of strength of will, hawk-like powers of observation and an unshakeable belief in her own righteousness. Against such powers, mere boys stood helpless. Clenched fists relaxed, arms dropped to sides. Boots, lifted in the very act of kicking, returned to the floor. Paper darts fell, unthrown. As the silence spread, the boys began shuffling back to their seats. They did not look at each other. Nor did they smile. There is no joy in a total rout. Rachel Lynde had conquered without firing a shot.

She did not gloat over her victory. She began merely by warning them that she was a disciple of the principle "spare the rod and spoil the child."

"I want at all times," she continued, "to see your two feet planted firmly on the floor and your two hands folded on the desk. Except, of course, when you are answering a question. Remember, when I ask a question, I expect an answer. I am noted," she could not resist adding, "for that."

Then she rolled up her sleeves and took attendance.

As she did so, Felix King listened and worried. Jimmy Spencer had not turned up for Sunday school, and Felix was not sure what to do about it.

Several weeks ago, when Felix had gone fishing instead of attending Sunday school, Jimmy Spencer had covered for him. When the teacher had read out Felix's name, Jimmy had simply called out "Present, sir!" and no one had been the wiser.

The teacher at that time had been a timid, ineffectual little man, unable to control his own twitches, let alone a class of rambunctious boys. Now instinct warned Felix there would be no pulling the wool over Mrs. Lynde's eyes. Yet loyalty to Jimmy bade him to try to cover for his absent friend.

Felix glanced over at his cousin, Andrew King, his senior by several years. Shielding his face behind the lid of his desk, he mouthed his question to Andrew.

What should I do about Jimmy Spencer?

Andrew shrugged in response, his face

expressing the same perplexity Felix felt.

"Felix King?"

So absorbed was Felix in his dilemma, that he barely heard Mrs. Lynde call his name.

"I said, *Felix King.*"

Felix jumped, bumping his head against the lid of his desk. "Ouch! Present, Mrs. Lynde," he squawked.

Mrs. Lynde droned on. Felix squirmed in his seat. Soon she would reach the "S"s. Should he risk mimicking Jimmy's voice? he wondered. Would he get away with it?

"Jimmy Spencer?"

Felix's voice sounded like a mouse caught in a trap with a mouthful of cheese. "Present, Mrs. Lynde."

There was an ominous pause, followed by a few suppressed titters.

Then, with heavy emphasis: "Would James Spencer please stand up?"

Felix retreated behind the desk lid, his face flushed, his heart thumping. He knew when he was beaten.

A silence fell. Mrs. Lynde glared around the room.

"Who is Jimmy Spencer and where does he live?"

The silence deepened. Felix did not dare look up. Andrew's head was buried in a book.

With an unerring instinct for the weakest link in the chain of defense, Mrs. Lynde strode over to Clive Rupert, the class goody-goody. She stared down at him, her arms folded.

"I repeat: Who is Jimmy Spencer and where does he live?"

It took only a few seconds for Clive to crumble. "He's the hired boy for Alexander Abraham, out on the White Sands Road," he croaked.

Mrs. Lynde committed the name and address to memory.

"Then I believe I shall have to pay Mr. Alexander Abraham a visit," she replied, before moving briskly on to the "T"s.

The following day Rachel Lynde donned her second-best brown suit, a silk shirtwaist, her gray visiting gloves and her hat with the tiny glazed oranges pinned to the hatband.

"I am off to White Sands Road to inquire why Mr. Abraham has not sent his hired boy to Sunday school," she informed Marilla.

"Not Mr. Alexander Abraham, surely?" inquired Marilla, putting down her teacup with unusual speed.

"And why not, pray?"

A glimmer of mirth appeared in Marilla's eyes. "In that case, you may have to prepare yourself for the possibility that Mr. Abraham will not appreciate your interest, Rachel."

"Whatever do you mean?"

"Mr. Abraham has...ah...a singular aversion to women. No woman has been known to set foot inside his house since his sister Mathilda died, twenty years ago."

"You don't mean to say his sister was Mathilda Abraham? Why, I remember her. She was known throughout Avonlea as a fine house-keeper. I heard she scrubbed that kitchen floor every second day."

"He hasn't taken kindly to visitors ever since Mathilda died. Hetty King told me he once swore that if a woman ever so much as set foot in his yard, he'd chase her out with a pitchfork."

Rachel Lynde set her jaw. A glint Marilla rec-ognized only too well flashed in her eyes.

"Well, you can mark my words, Marilla," she snapped. "No man will chase *me* out of anywhere with a farm implement."

Marilla continued to drink her tea long after the screen door had slammed shut behind Rachel. If it must come to a pitched battle, she reasoned, Rachel Lynde and Alexander Abraham were well-matched opponents. Since there was nothing she could do to prevent a confrontation, she might as well enjoy the calm before the storm, for storm there certainly would be.

Chapter Three

At almost exactly the same time as Rachel Lynde was preparing to beard Mr. Abraham in his den, Sara and her three King cousins were setting out for the same Mr. Abraham's barn. Sara was staying at the King Farm while Aunt Hetty and Aunt Olivia were on a trip to Charlottetown.

It had taken Felix some time and much argument before the others had agreed to accompany him on his mission to warn Jimmy Spencer that Rachel Lynde was after him.

Felicity had been quite decided about *not* going. "I really can't see why you're making such a fuss over a hired hand," she had said dismissively when Felix first suggested the idea.

"Don't you see? I owe Jimmy a favor," Felix had retorted. "He stood in for me that time I went trouting in the brook instead of going to Sunday school."

"You mean you skipped Sunday school,

Felix?" Ten-year-old Cecily's eyes were two round saucers in her round little face.

"Sure I did. But don't you breathe a word of it to Mother or Father."

"Really Felix, you seem to think skipping Sunday school makes you some kind of dare-devil," sniffed Felicity, who was behaving exactly like someone who had climbed out of the wrong side of bed that morning.

At first Cecily had also refused to go, because of old Mr. Abraham's reputation around Avonlea as a mean old man.

"I'd be much too scared of bumping into Him," she had whispered, as though Mr. Abraham were God or the Devil. "I'll only go if Felicity holds my hand the whole time."

Needless to say, the idea of encountering the reclusive Mr. Abraham seemed to Sara the most interesting aspect of the enterprise. She never failed to be intrigued by the variety and vagaries of human nature.

Finally they reached a consensus. They would go because Felix felt honor-bound to find Jimmy. But they would not remain long on the premises. They would seek out Jimmy Spencer, warn him of Mrs. Lynde's imminent visitation and leave. Felicity grudgingly agreed to hold Cecily's hand

throughout the entire trip, but she gave in with
such bad grace that a pall had settled over the
excursion before they had taken their first step.

Felicity's temper did not improve as the day
wore on. Truth to tell, her bad mood was one that
the family had grown used to of late, ever since
Sara first arrived.

As the eldest and most striking of the three
King children, Felicity was accustomed to
attracting attention and admiration wherever she
went. Tall for thirteen, with a pink-and-white
complexion, she wore her long, thick, chestnut
hair streaming down her back. Already an
accomplished seamstress, she had developed a
reputation amongst the girls of Avonlea as their
resident expert on fashion and household arts.
To her they flocked for advice about which
gloves to wear to a wedding, the best method of
getting dough to rise and the neatest way to turn
a sleeve.

In short, Felicity was accustomed to such lime-
light as Avonlea had to offer, and she had no
desire to share it. Yet with Sara's arrival on the
Island, Felicity felt her monopoly threatened. Not
that Sara was prettier than Felicity. Sara could not
boast of Felicity's conventional good looks. Small
for her twelve years, with a pointed white face in

which the eyes seemed almost too large, and a
tumble of pale hair, there was something elfin,
almost otherworldly about Sara. Her face reflected
a vivid inward life. One could not look at Sara and
call her beautiful, as one might describe Felicity.
Yet one could not look once at Sara's face and ever
forget it.

Sara Stanley had grown up in Montreal, the
imaginative only daughter of a wealthy financier.
Her mother had died when Sara was little more
than a baby. When her father's business collapsed
amidst rumors of a financial scandal, Sara had
been sent to Prince Edward Island, to live with
her mother's family, the Kings of Avonlea.

Unlike Felicity, Sara had never in her whole
life baked bread or sewn a seam. Nor had she
ever devoured the *Family Guide* from cover to
cover, as Felicity did regularly. The *Family Guide*,
a manual of manners, useful in all matters
domestic and worldly, was Felicity's secular
Bible. She had committed whole sections from its
pages to memory. Sara, on the other hand, found
it difficult to commit anything to memory except
poetry.

But if Sara had arrived in Avonlea untutored
in the domestic arts, she brought with her an
array of other skills, which up to then had been

unknown, and thus unvalued, by Felicity.

For one thing, Sara could tell a fine story. Now this may not, at first glance, seem any great gift. But to hear Sara tell a story was to be transported back into days of old, when the whole of civilization depended for its entertainment on the spoken word. When Sara told a tale, princesses and princes, goblins and trolls, appeared before the children's eyes, as though summoned by magic. Her voice became their voices, the voices of ancient royalty, of nymphs and dryads, specters and spirits. She made their sorrows and loves, their actions and gestures, her own. And although her stories told of creatures from distant lands and times, they seemed familiar to the children, as though they recognized, dimly, something of themselves in the tales.

Sara made imagination take wing in a way Felicity had never known possible. It was this gift that had earned her the name "the Story Girl."

Sara had another gift, one which the fashion-conscious Felicity resented even more. It was this which was on Felicity's mind now, as she strode grumpily through the grass towards Alexander Abraham's farm. She was still smarting from her experience in church the day before.

What had happened was this.

On Saturday, Felicity had devoted most of her day to retrimming her best Sunday hat. From the peddler who appeared in Avonlea from time to time, she had bought a splendid piece of broad velvet ribbon. All her precious egg-money had gone on that ribbon, which was of the deepest midnight-blue.

With her mother's help, she removed the slightly faded turquoise cotton band from the crown of the hat and replaced it with the velvet. Then, using the daintiest of stitching, she sewed two narrower, pale-blue ribbons onto the velvet, outlining it, top and bottom. These ribbons were longer. They tied into a bow at the back and fell in a graceful slope onto Felicity's hair.

After she had finished pushing her reluctant needle through the tough straw, Felicity's poor fingers were bruised and punctured. Eye strain had caused a tiny network of red veins to appear in her left eye and her back ached from bending over her work. Yet she felt buoyed up by the knowledge that she had accomplished what she set out to do. In place of her worn and faded old hat, she now had one that looked gloriously new. When she thought of the effect it would have in church the next day, all her fatigue dissipated and she positively glowed.

And indeed, that Sunday morning as she entered church, Felicity felt like a queen wearing her crown for the first time. With downcast eyes she entered the King family pew, expecting to hear murmurs of approval from the girls in the surrounding pews. When not one single subdued compliment reached her ears, she raised her eyes and saw at once the reason for the silence.

Sara was walking down the nave, wearing a simple white-and-yellow dress. She wore no hat. Instead, she had pinned two or three daisies in her fair hair.

The morning sun spilled through the colored windows and onto Sara, so that she seemed to drift in a stream of light. The white-gold hair, the white and yellow daisies, the pale skin, the honey-colored dress, all seemed to blend into one natural, shimmering whole.

Dragging her eyes away, Felicity glanced at her friends and schoolmates. Without exception they were all staring at Sara. They looked bewitched, bedazzled. And the worst thing about it, Felicity thought, wanting to burst into tears, was that it all looked so *effortless*. She knew Sara had no idea of the effect her entrance had caused. She had not planned it. She was simply being Sara, a Sara who sometimes aroused in her elder cousin a resentment amounting to fury.

As the memory of yesterday's humiliation returned, Felicity glared at Sara, who ambled, all unknowing, ahead of her, dreamily picking buttercups.

"Everyone at church yesterday thought you looked mighty foolish, Sara Stanley," she burst out. "You looked like you were showing off."

Felix looked over at his sister. He was two years younger than Felicity, but he could on occasion be alarmingly perceptive about her feelings.

"You're just jealous 'cause no one noticed your fancy hat," he remarked.

Sara turned. "I noticed it. After church, when you were standing by Aunt Janet, I thought the blue velvet set off your eyes quite wonderfully. You made me think of lapis lazuli and faraway seas."

Now Felicity of all people knew a compliment when she heard one. She might have had no idea that lapis lazuli was a prized gem of brightest blue. Nor did faraway seas sound as entrancing to her as they did to Sara. But the general tone of the remark was flattering, she could tell.

Even such generous words, however, failed to smooth her ruffled vanity. The truth was that Felicity had worked herself into such a lather of rage that it would take more than words to rinse her clean. The venom in her response was startling, even to her.

"Well, I thought you looked perfectly ridiculous, Sara. Flowers in your hair in church. What *will* you think of next?"

"I don't see why it should be all right to wear flowers on your dress and not in your hair," objected Sara, pointing to the floral pattern on Felicity's pinafore.

"Oh you don't, don't you? Well in that case, I dare you to wear that old funeral wreath on your hair!"

Tucked away in a corner of the field they were passing stood a small family graveyard, most of its headstones weathered and crumbling. Had it not been for the small wreath propped up against one of the more erect gravestones, a casual observer might have been forgiven for thinking the whole place abandoned. It was at this wreath that Felicity now pointed.

Sara stared at her in disbelief. Felicity surely couldn't expect her to steal someone else's funeral wreath. But this, and nothing less, was clearly what Felicity did expect.

"Go on. I dare you. Stick those flowers on your head!"

Sara took a step forward. Cecily pulled her back. "Don't do it, Sara. You mustn't ask her to, Felicity!"

The wreath was made up of once sweet-smelling grasses, intertwined with small dried flowers: rosebuds and marigolds, daisies and bachelor's buttons. Sara had no idea how long it had lain there in the quiet field. Someone had lovingly picked those flowers and woven them into this circle of remembrance, someone who wanted to honor a departed loved one. How could she possibly take it away?

"See? It's all talk with you, Sara Stanley. You'd no more wear those filthy old flowers on your head than you'd wear a chamber pot!"

This was too much for Sara. The flowers may have been dry and a little dusty, but they were not filthy. They were a token of real affection. She was not going to let Felicity insult them. Stooping, she bent her head close to the tomb.

"Don't worry. I'll return them," she whispered to the silent stone.

In one swift, graceful motion she picked up the wreath and placed it on her head. Then she walked proudly back to her cousins. The wreath, with its faded daisies and russet leaves, framed her elfin face. Around her neck hung a glowing yellow chain of buttercups, woven as she had picked them along the way.

Instead of looking out of place and silly, as Felicity had hoped, she seemed in harmony with the quiet place. She looked, thought Felicity furiously, as though she were a spirit of the meadows.

Chapter Four

Felix turned and walked impatiently away from the graveyard. He had had about enough of his elder sister's bad mood.

"We've got to hurry, Felicity. If I don't warn Jimmy, Rachel Lynde will catch him. And then the fat'll be in the fire. Why, he might even get a hiding from old man Abraham!"

In less than five minutes, the children reached the Abraham farm.

As soon as they laid eyes on the house, they could tell it belonged to someone with a reputation for crustiness. Neglect was written all over it. Weeds grew up to the very door. The woodwork cried out thirstily for a lick of paint. What blinds remained hung crooked and torn. The windows wore a thick curtain of dust.

Felicity eyed it with distaste. "It's plain to see there's no woman around that place," she sniffed.

"Yeah, but take a look at the barn. That's a mighty nice barn!" replied Felix, who had inherited the King talent for farming.

Sara gave no thought to the barn. The sight of the house, with its blank windows, had aroused in her an almost forgotten memory.

As a small child she had once journeyed on her own from Quebec City to Montreal by train. She remembered sitting alone in the carriage while night fell. As the train creaked slowly through the outskirts of the city, she had been able to gaze from her carriage into the grimy windows of the houses huddled close to the tracks.

She had seen there a life she had never experienced before: families sitting around their evening meal, mothers reading to their children or simply holding them on their laps. To the lonely child, each window seemed to offer a glimpse into a crowded family life she had never known. The vision was enhanced by the warm, amber-tinged glow from the lamp that lit each room.

At one window, Sara had seen a mother reaching up to close the curtain. Behind her a man moved, a child in each arm, another on his back. They were dressed for bed. The man was twirling them around, plunging and rearing as though he were a horse, while the children laughed and shrieked with delight.

Then the woman pulled the curtain shut.

The sight had stayed in Sara's mind long afterwards. If she had been able to paint, she would have painted that scene of a happy family, glimpsed from the outer dark.

The darkness of Mr. Abraham's windows reminded her of that scene and of her own feeling of loneliness. She felt a surge of sympathy for the old bachelor, whom everyone seemed to fear.

"His house looks so sad, don't you think?" she whispered. "With its windows so bare and bleak."

"Reminds me of something dead, with its eyes picked out," replied Felix, who had had enough discussion for one day. "Now come on! I've gotta look in the barn. I'll bet that's where Jimmy is."

But Jimmy Spencer was not to be found in the barn. Nor could they run him to ground in any of the small sheds grouped nearby. Puzzled, the children made their way back towards the house.

"Maybe Rachel Lynde's already been here," worried Felix. "Maybe she's dragged him back to town and locked him in the church, just so he won't miss next Sunday."

"Does that mean we can go home now?" piped up Cecily, who had been remarkably silent for some time, in mortal fear that Mr. Alexander Abraham might appear at any moment in a puff of smoke. "*Please* let's go home. I'm awful scared of Him!"

"I don't think you need to be afraid of him, Cecily," said Sara. "He's probably not nearly as frightening as people say. In fact I think he sounds quite interesting. I'd rather like to meet him."

Felicity rolled her eyes heavenward. "You think you can make friends with just about anyone, don't you, Sara Stanley!"

"Not with old man Abraham you can't," commented Felix. "Everyone says he hates women."

"Well, I'm not a woman yet," answered Sara, with irrefutable logic. "So even if it's true that he hates women, he'd have no reason to hate me."

"Very well then." Felicity's ability to put up with Sara's irritating self-confidence a moment longer had come to an abrupt end. "Go and make friends with him, go on. I dare you. Just march right up to that front door and knock. *Go on!*"

Sara did not hesitate. Knocking on someone's front door seemed a trifling matter, compared to robbing a grave of its funeral wreath.

Without a word, she jumped onto the front porch and strode to the door. Lifting the tarnished brass knocker, she let it fall heavily back into place. All this was accomplished so quickly that the others scarcely had time to realize what she was doing. As the loud knocking reverberated through the house, they scattered wildly, looking for places to hide.

Just as Sara was lifting the knocker a second time, a large dog bounded around the corner of the front porch and headed straight towards her. Sara stared at him curiously, waiting for him to bark. But for some reason, the dog remained silent. It ran noiselessly in her direction, its purpose and attitude a mystery.

"Just keep calm," hissed Felix from his hiding place in the bushes to one side of the porch. "Don't let him see you're frightened."

"I'm not frightened," replied Sara calmly. "I can make friends with anyone, human or animal."

Stretching out her arm, she attempted to stroke the dog's brown head. The dog jerked away and looked up at her quickly. Then, as though something about her had convinced him she meant well, he bowed his head and submitted to her hand.

Again, Sara's confidence set Felicity's teeth on edge.

"I dare you to go into the house," she called out. "Anyone can see there's no one home."

"I can't go into someone's house, Felicity! You're being silly."

With her arm around the dog, who by now was wagging his tail, Sara descended the porch steps.

"I am *not* being silly." Felicity stamped her foot, her eyes blazing. "All you have to do is go inside, count to ten and come back out. There's nothing to it. I dare you, Sara."

Sara sighed. Felicity seemed to be behaving in such an odd fashion this morning. She glanced over at Cecily. The ten-year-old stood rigidly beside her elder sister, her face pale, her thumb jammed into her mouth.

Cecily had almost grown out of the habit of sucking her thumb. Sara knew that she only reverted to this childish practice when she was well and truly terrified. Perhaps she should indulge Felicity's whim after all. The sooner she did, the sooner Felicity would be satisfied. Then they could all go home and let poor Cecily recover her wits.

"All right, I'll do it. I'll go inside."

This time, as Sara approached the dirty front

door, she trod on a rotten floorboard. It gave way with a sudden crack. For a moment, her foot dangled in the nothingness that lurks under every front porch. Trying not to panic, she held onto the door and jerked her foot upwards and out. A huge sigh of relief escaped her lips. Briefly, she had been unable to suppress images of spiders and hungry bats nibbling at her imprisoned foot.

Moving more cautiously now, she turned the handle. But the door, swollen with damp or age, was either locked or stuck. It refused to budge.

"I can't get in," she called back. "The door seems to be locked."

"Try a window, then." Felicity was implacable. "There's an open one on this side of the house."

Sara was about to protest when she remembered Cecily's stricken face. Doing her best to avoid any further encounters with rotten floorboards, she ran lightly along the front porch, down the steps and over to the spot where Felicity stood.

A large, low-branching plum tree leaned towards one side of the house. Looking up, Sara could see an open window on the second floor. What seemed, to her inexpert eye, a tolerably strong branch reached towards the window, almost touching it.

"Go on! I dare you."

Felicity's cheeks were flushed. Sara wondered whether she were ill.

"I'm not going to argue with you, Felicity, but I think you're being extremely silly."

Felicity's response was to stick out her tongue.

With a sigh of exasperation, Sara began to climb the tree.

Chapter Five

If Sara had looked down towards the lane as she climbed, she might have spied Mrs. Lynde advancing briskly towards Mr. Abraham's house. But Sara was too taken with the verdant beauty around her to look down at the pedestrian earth. Above her, she could see an azure sky framed by a fringe of leaves. Through a sweet-smelling branch to her left, she caught a glimpse of the brighter blue of the sea. It sparkled as it danced, seeming to beckon her invitingly.

All her worries about Cecily's fear and Felicity's strange mood seeped out of her soul as a great surge of delight in the wonder of the world swept in.

"It's so beautiful up here," she sighed to herself. "A symphony in greens and blues."

Below her, Felix almost danced with impatience.

"Would you just stop goggling and get inside!" he implored. "Old man Abraham might come back at any moment!"

Hardly were the words out of his mouth when the dog raised its brown head and cocked its ears. Uttering a low growl, it disappeared round the corner towards the front of the house. The children stiffened in fear.

"Now we're in for it," whispered Felix. "He's back! And he's gonna go raving mad when he sees us!"

Around the corner, out of sight, the dog could be heard barking furiously.

"If it's Mr. Abraham who's back, then why would his dog bark?" wondered Felicity.

As they stared at each other in terror, unsure whether to run or stay, an unmistakable voice assaulted their ears.

"Get down! Get DOWN, you loathsome creature!" it roared.

Fearful bangings and rappings shook the side of the porch.

The children clutched each other in shock.

"It's Mrs. Lynde!" croaked Felicity.

"It's Rachel Lynde!" hissed Felix up the tree to where Sara crouched precariously on a branch. "Get down this minute, Sara! If she catches us here, we'll never hear the last of it!"

Whoever claimed that the devil you know is better than the devil you don't, had obviously never met Rachel Lynde. As far as the children were concerned, they would rather have been trapped by an unknown Mr. Abraham than encounter the all-too-familiar wrath of Mrs. Lynde.

The one exception to this rule was Cecily, who was too young to have ever experienced the rough side of Rachel's tongue. Poor Cecily had heard so much whispered talk about the fearsome Mr. Abraham that he loomed in her imagination like a cross between the Ghost of Christmas Past and the Devil incarnate. Could anybody, even Rachel Lynde, possibly be worse than Him? Her whole body shook with terror as she squeezed her elder sister's hand.

"What should we do, Felicity?" she gasped.

"Do? Why, we have to run. Get down, Sara, for Heaven's sake!"

"I'm coming as fast as I can. I—Ohh, no!"

In edging towards the trunk from one of the outer branches, Sara had caught the back of her pinafore on a jutting limb. Try as she might, she could not budge it.

"Please, Felix! Climb up and help me!" she implored.

"All right. I'm coming. I'm coming!"

Fear lent unaccustomed swiftness to Felix's ascent. "Gosh, Sara!" he puffed as he climbed. "I hope you'll think twice the next time before you accept one of Felicity's silly dares."

The same thought had occurred to Sara, who did not reply. Her earlier exhilaration had vanished, replaced by a growing feeling of dread.

The wind had risen. Under its uneven pressure the branches rocked back and forth. Leaves rattled harshly all around her, blotting out sight of the sea. Her stomach churned in rhythm with the motion of the tree. Although she was relieved to see Felix approaching closer, she feared his added weight might place too much of a strain on the branch where she was caught.

"I don't think you sh—" she began.

But it was too late. With a loud cracking sound, the long branch snapped in half, propelling both Sara and Felix onto the small balcony underneath Mr. Abraham's second-floor window. One minute they were clinging to the branch for dear life, the next they had been flung onto the balcony, as though by an enormous fist.

Sara had fallen close by the window. Hearing a moan, she picked herself up and raced over to Felix, who had landed half on and half off the balcony. His hands and arms clutched frantically at the shaking wood, while his feet kicked out into space.

Grabbing his arms, Sara managed to heave him over the side, where he lay on the floor, his eyes still closed in dread, his face working.

"It's all right, Felix. You're safe now," whispered Sara. She crouched down beside him, patting his head consolingly. "You can open your eyes and stand up."

As they clambered to their feet and looked cautiously over the rail, both children gasped in dismay, for there, far below them on the ground, broken and useless, in a heap of scattered leaves and broken twigs, lay their former means of escape. No longer could they climb down by way of the plum tree.

They were trapped on Mr. Abraham's balcony. Now they had no choice but to sneak inside his house.

Chapter Six

As she approached the farm from the lane, Rachel Lynde had been forced to concede that she was favorably impressed by the condition of Mr. Abraham's barns. Rachel's father had always maintained that you could take the measure of a farmer by the shape of his barns. Mr. Abraham's were large, well-painted and trim.

"Credit where credit is due," she thought to herself. "He may be a woman-hater, but I'd say he knows how to run a farm. Still, they say you can't judge a book by its cover, and maybe you shouldn't judge a farmer by his barns either, no matter what my poor father used to say."

And indeed, when she caught a glimpse of the house, she was glad she had not been taken in by the barns.

"I declare, that house has woman-hater written all over it!" she exclaimed, taking stock of its drab, neglected appearance. "It's plain to see no woman has set foot in that house for donkey's years."

Fired with the proud knowledge that she was about to thrust herself where no woman had dared to tread for almost a quarter of a century, Rachel advanced upon the front porch. But as she drew nearer, she was startled by ferocious growls and barks. No dog was visible, yet the growls sounded alarmingly realistic. Surely Mr. Abraham would not stoop so low as to imitate a dog in order to scare women away? Rachel snorted. The idea was ludicrous. Yet, Lord knows, a man like Mr. Abraham might resort to anything. Wouldn't she love to catch him at it! Think of the fun she would have telling the neighbors of his foolishness.

The next minute the smug smile was wiped from Rachel Lynde's face, for around the corner of the porch tore a dog, the likes of which she had never seen in her whole life.

To say it was an ugly dog would be to speak kindly. It was just about the plainest animal Rachel had ever encountered in a lifetime of avoiding homely canines. Large and loose, floppy and clumsy, it flashed around the porch towards her, its dirty brown coat stained with black patches. Its jaws opened and shut with heart-stopping efficiency, revealing enormous pointed teeth. For a bulky animal, it moved with surprising speed. It darted and feinted around Rachel like a matador baiting a bull.

With her foot on the lowest porch step, Rachel gasped in disbelief. Could this hound of hell really be pointing those horrible teeth at *her*?

One snap at the hem of her skirt convinced

her that she was indeed the target of its wrath. Abandoning all pretence of dignity, she scuttled up the steps towards the front door, the dog hot on her heels.

"Get down! Get DOWN, you loathsome creature!" she screamed. But still the dog came on, its jaws working, saliva trickling from its mouth.

With a sob of gratitude, Rachel remembered her umbrella. Lifting it high she brought it down as hard as she could on the railing of the front porch. Again and again, she walloped the wood. But instead of intimidating the dog, the noise only seemed to send it into further paroxysms of barking.

"Saints-a-mercy! The beast will tear me limb from limb! What'll I do? What'll I *do*?" she moaned.

Flinging away her umbrella, she grabbed the railing with both hands and attempted to clamber over it. But the complicated corset, into which she had laced herself that afternoon restricted her movements. Rachel could no more have climbed that railing than she could have draped herself in scarlet silk. Yet she refused to recognize defeat. After much struggling, she managed to get one foot wedged halfway up between the slats, while with the other she attempted to bounce her large frame up and over the fence.

This action seemed to delight the dog, whose jaws gaped dangerously close to Rachel's ample posterior.

"Leave me alone, you vile, wicked beast! Get away, get away, get AWAY!"

She kicked out wildly with her free foot. The vile beast dodged, snatched a corner of her second-best skirt in its teeth, and attempted to drag it off the porch, with or without Rachel inside it.

Emitting a squawk of pure despair, Rachel leapt from the railing towards the front door.

There was a huge crash, followed by the sickening sound of rotten floorboards giving way. One of Rachel's feet buried itself in the porch, while the other landed squarely on the base of the front door. The rest of Rachel followed after it. Under this ferocious assault, the door had no choice but to give way. With a shuddering sigh it swung inward, sending Rachel careening forward onto the hall floor.

There was a stunned silence. The fall seemed to have knocked all the air out of Rachel. She felt like a huge, deflated balloon. In the silence, a small glazed orange bounced from her hat and rolled across the dark floor like a tiny bright marble. Her hat tried to follow but encountered an obstacle in the shape of her nose, which was pressed against a dusty carpet. Her left foot remained stubbornly outside on the porch; she had no idea where her right one had vanished to.

Looking up from this ungainly posture, she perceived a man staring down at her. His face expressed shocked disbelief.

Rachel glared at him with the one eye not smothered in carpet.

"Good morning to you, Mr. Abraham," she snapped. "Did no one ever inform you it is rude to stare?"

Chapter Seven

In general appearance, Mr. Alexander Abraham resembled nothing less than a strange combination of his dog and his house.

He had the same floppy looseness of limb and skin as the animal outside. His eyes, too, were large and brown, with a faintly puzzled look. Even from her disadvantaged position, Rachel could see that the shirt he wore lacked several buttons. Something about it—rumpled and collarless as it was—reminded her of the crooked blinds and dusty windows that lent his house its unkempt appearance.

Yet the barns were there too. There was no denying the barns. They were present in the straightness of his shoulders and the cut of his shabby black jacket. Give that jacket a decent sponging down, followed by a brisk brushing up, she thought, and it could still hold its own with the best of them. As for his hair, well, it was wild and white and floated in wisps around his head, like dandelion seeds in a summer breeze.

Mrs. Lynde could not deny there was something downright distinguished about white hair in men—but not when it reminded her of those pesky dandelions which threatened to take over the lawn at Green Gables.

Propelled by the thought of thousands of weeds pleading to be rooted out, Mrs. Lynde pushed herself up from the rug with her arms. A cloud of dust rose with her. Mr. Abraham backed hastily away. The stunned look fled from his face, replaced by an angry one.

"What in Heaven's name do you think you're doing in my house, woman!" he thundered. "You're trespassing! Do you realize that?"

Rachel scrambled to her feet. With difficulty, she adjusted her hat, which seemed to have pirouetted several times on her head. A few more oranges broke away from the band and bumped forlornly down her nose, to disappear, perhaps forever, into the dusty carpet.

"Trespassing!" exclaimed Rachel, with as much dignity as she could muster. "Why, I'll have you know, Mr. Abraham, that I've a good mind to report you and that beast of yours to the Carmody magistrate. You should be prosecuted for having such an animal. He might have maimed me for life."

"That damage, I'm afraid, madam, was clearly inflicted at birth. Now get out! You hear me? O-U-T!"

"Mr. Abraham!"

After such a trying morning, Rachel felt no obligation to mind her manners. If he was going to raise his voice to her, why, she would raise hers right back.

"Mr. Abraham, would you listen to me for one minute?"

"Confound it, woman! I am not deaf. Although perhaps *you* are. Do you not understand the King's English? I said get out!"

"Don't flatter yourself for one minute I came to see *you*!" fumed Rachel. "*You* are the last man on earth I would choose to visit. I came to see Jimmy Spencer and see him I will."

Mr. Abraham had opened his mouth to

deliver an angry reply. Now he shut it again with a snap. A cagey look crept into his eyes.

"What...who?"

"Where is Jimmy Spencer, Mr. Abraham? I shall not leave this spot until I have seen him."

"Jimmy's not here," answered Mr. Abraham quickly. "He...um...he no longer works on this farm."

For some reason his face reminded her of Felix King's during roll call at Sunday school the previous day. Felix had been up to something, she had felt sure of it. She strongly suspected Mr. Abraham was up to something too. The trouble was, she had no idea what that something might be.

Rachel's brow furrowed. She raked Mr. Abraham with her gaze, but he refused to meet her eye. Instead, he stooped and picked up a glazed orange from the thicket of carpet. He dropped it into Rachel's palm.

"Take up your fruit, woman, and go!"

Rachel extracted the hat decoration from a tangle of carpet fluff and popped it into her bag. Her second-best hat was well and truly ruined. But her mind could not grapple with hats at that moment. Her mind was on Mr. Abraham and his suspicious behavior.

If Jimmy had genuinely left Mr. Abraham's

employment, then there was no need for her to
stay. Nor had she any desire to stay a moment
longer than was necessary. Yet something was
amiss. Her bones insisted upon it. Rachel felt
many things in her bones, apart from the damp.
She was noted for that.

Snapping her bag shut, she came to a decision.

"In that case, Mr. Abraham," she said, "I shall not
trouble you any further." Inwardly, she had resolved
to search the barns thoroughly on her way out.

"I think that would be the wisest thing,"
agreed Mr. Abraham. He spoke nervously. "Please
leave as quietly and as quickly as you can."

His tone puzzled Rachel. It sounded neither
threatening nor hostile, merely as though he were
unsure about the outcome of his statement.

Turning towards the back door, he motioned
Rachel to follow him.

Rachel, however, had no intention of leaving
by the back entrance. With a haughty sniff, she
drew herself up to her full height.

"Mr. Abraham," she said loftily. "I am not
accustomed to being shown the back door. I am no
thief who comes in the night. I am a respectable
widow. Now you kindly call that hell-hound of
yours to heel and I shall leave the way I came. By
the front door, if you please."

Mr. Abraham seemed about to protest, but thought better of it. He raised his fingers to his lips and gave a piercing whistle. The dog bounded inside, completely ignoring his former victim, and rubbed himself like a kitten against Mr. Abraham's knees.

Rachel felt like strangling the beast with her bare hands. Instead, she dismissed them both with a curt nod and strode out through the front door.

As she stepped onto the porch, a buggy rattled up the driveway and pulled to a halt in front of her. Inside sat two men, Constable Jeffries and Dr. Blair. Behind her she heard Mr. Abraham give a great moan of despair.

"Confound it, woman! You're too late. Now you've really set the cat among the pigeons!"

Chapter Eight

For what seemed like hours, Felicity and Cecily had waited in the bushes by the side of Mr. Abraham's house, hardly daring to breathe. In an agony of fear, they had watched as the branch had broken off and tumbled Sara and Felix onto the second-floor balcony. They had seen Felix's feet search frantically for a foothold and find none.

At that moment, staring up at the soles of their brother's boots, both girls had remembered his sweet nature and easy laugh. All his tiresome habits were entirely forgotten as they clutched each other and prayed he would not fall to his death.

Then Sara had appeared by the balcony rail and pulled their brother to safety. They could not see what happened next, but after a few moments, two frightened faces had appeared over the rail and stared in disbelief at the remnants of branch on the ground below. Shaking her head, Sara had said something to Felix, and the two faces had disappeared.

Down below, the two girls waited in silence. Felicity could only assume that Felix and Sara had decided to climb in through Mr. Abraham's window and make their way down through the house to freedom.

What if Mrs. Lynde caught them? Or worse, what if Mr. Abraham were still inside the house, waiting in deceitful silence for the children to enter?

Cecily's lower lip quivered. "What if Mr. Abraham pounces on them?" she wailed. "They may never come out alive!"

It seemed to Felicity that the whole situation had grown dangerously out of control. She did not want to think about her role in what was rapidly turning into a disaster. Doing her best to keep her voice steady, she tried to reassure her sister. After all, she was still the eldest. She was still in charge, no matter how small and guilty she might feel.

"It's highly unlikely Mr. Abraham's there, Cecily. After all, we did knock and he didn't answer."

She was surprised by how calm she sounded.

"And then Sara tried the door, remember? She thought it was locked. He's probably gone away for the day."

"But Felicity! If the front door's locked, how will Sara and Felix get out?"

"They'll open it from the inside, silly. You'll see."

This seemed to reassure Cecily. Taking her by the hand, Felicity crept around the house towards the front porch.

It was at this point that she saw the opened door and heard Rachel Lynde's voice raised in argument with that of a man. The man sounded hoarse with fury. He was roaring at Rachel that she was trespassing, ordering her out of his house.

It was Alexander Abraham, and if he dared to speak to Mrs. Lynde, of all people, in such tones, what would he not do to two defenseless children?

Chapter Nine

Up on the second floor, Sara and Felix heard the raised voices too. They stood there in the dark, musty room, which seemed more like an excuse for storing jumble than a bedroom, and listened to the anger rising up from below. Before Rachel Lynde ever addressed him by his name, both children knew the man's voice must belong to Mr. Abraham.

They said nothing. They could almost feel each other's fear. There was no point in speaking.

They would have to creep downstairs and try to sneak out the front or back door. They both knew that. But when, and how? Imagine if the dog found them first, sniffed them out of their hiding place upstairs. Imagine if Mr. Abraham hated girls as much as he was said to hate women. Imagine if—Sara shook herself. Too much imagination could turn even the bravest heroine into a jellyfish, she decided.

Putting her finger to her lips to warn Felix not to speak, she tiptoed into the upstairs hallway and leaned over the banister. She was just in time to catch Mr. Abraham's exclamation of dismay as the buggy pulled up outside in the driveway.

In another second, Dr. Blair's heavy tread sounded on the porch steps.

He, too, seemed angry.

"Mrs. Lynde," he snapped. "Have you no sense? What in Heaven's name are you doing here?"

"I beg your pardon, Dr. Blair," retorted Rachel, feeling as if all the world were conspiring against her. "I had no idea I must first ask your permission before paying a call on a Sunday school scholar."

Behind the doctor, Rachel could see the burly form of Constable Jeffries. For some reason he had not followed Dr. Blair inside, but was keeping his distance from the house, watching it nervously, as though it might at any minute spring up and attack him.

"I would ask you to remember, Doctor," she continued, "that I am a widow of a certain age and social standing. If such as I cannot visit a pupil without causing a minor scandal in Avonlea, then Heaven help those younger and less proper than myself."

Dr. Blair was no longer listening to Mrs. Lynde. He had turned his attention to Mr. Abraham.

"Perhaps I did not make it clear to you how grave the situation is, Mr. Abraham," he said reproachfully. "I thought you had given me your solemn promise you would not let anyone into this house."

"I didn't let her in, man," growled Mr. Abraham. "Honest to Pete, the confounded woman flung herself right through that door. Locked and all as it was. Without so much as a by-your-leave. I found her on the floor here, groveling at my feet."

Rachel Lynde blushed scarlet. If looks could have killed, Mr. Abraham would have keeled over with a stiletto in his heart.

"Would someone kindly explain what is going on here? I declare, I have never felt so beleaguered in my whole life. I do not intend to remain here and have my integrity insulted one minute longer. Good day, gentlemen!"

Gathering the tatters of her dignity around her, she turned to leave.

Dr. Blair barred her way.

"I beg your pardon, Mrs. Lynde," he insisted, and there was something in his manner, that made Rachel listen to him, despite her extreme anxiety to be gone. "You are indeed mistaken if you think I meant to insult you, but I'm afraid I cannot now permit you to leave this place."

"Cannot permit me? Not leave this place? Explain yourself, Doctor!"

"I'm afraid, Mrs. Lynde, that Jimmy Spencer, who is Mr. Abraham's hired boy—"

"I know who Jimmy Spencer is, Doctor. Did I not inform you that I came here with the express intention of seeing him?"

"Jimmy Spencer has come down with the smallpox, Mrs. Lynde. I have just delivered him to the hospital in Charlottetown. His case, I'm sad to say, is grave. Since Mr. Abraham has been exposed to the disease, this house is under a fourteen-day quarantine. You will understand, I'm sure, that as you are now here, you will not be allowed to leave."

For a moment, Rachel's world spun dizzily. As soon as it righted itself, she turned in anger to Mr. Abraham, who stood silently by his dog.

"Why didn't you tell me, you cantankerous old fool?"

"Tell you? I did the kindest thing I could think of, woman. I tried to let you leave in happy ignorance. Perhaps that will teach you not to barge into a man's home without first asking permission."

"Ladies and gentlemen, please," implored Dr. Blair. "Let us not make the situation worse by behaving disagreeably. Now, let us sit down and I shall explain the laws of quarantine to you, calmly and rationally."

So saying, he led the way into Mr. Abraham's murky sitting room which, with its lopsided sofa and dust-laden furniture, seemed to Rachel to look more like the anteroom to purgatory than a gentleman's front parlor.

Upstairs, Sara and Felix stood aghast.

"They can't quarantine us with Mr. Abraham and Mrs. Lynde, c-c-can they?" whispered Felix. The mere thought made him shudder.

"Our only chance is to escape now. Quickly, while they're all in the parlor," replied Sara, doing her best to squash the feeling of panic mounting within her.

Felix swallowed. He knew she was right. If they didn't make a dash for it now, they might never get another opportunity. But his heart quailed at the thought of having to descend the stairs and sneak past the open parlor door.

"I'll make the stairs creak, I know I will!"

Normally, Felix never worried about his

tendency towards plumpness. It took a situation such as this to make him aware how each spare ounce of unnecessary weight increased the likelihood of an old stair tread complaining loudly.

Bending down, Sara tugged at his laces. "Take your boots off and carry them. Hurry!" she hissed.

For once Felix did as he was told without argument. As soon as the boots were off, he tied their laces together and strung them around his neck.

Sara preceded him to the head of the stairs.

"Tiptoe down. Pretend you're the wind skimming the steps. Fly as lightly and as quickly as you can. I'll get to the door first and hold it open for you. Good luck."

She kissed him solemnly on the cheek. Then she turned and started down. Felix followed.

He tried to pretend he was the wind. The trouble was, pretending did not come naturally to him. Where Sara could transform herself effortlessly into a witch or a butterfly, Felix found the mental strain almost insurmountable. Despite his most valiant efforts, he would remain stubbornly himself. As he hurried downstairs, he forced himself to concentrate.

He *could* imagine he was the wind, silent and

swift. Of course he could. He had only to stop worrying about the steps creaking. He had only to force his mind away from his feet.

Concentrating made him close his eyes. Closing his eyes made him stumble. As he stumbled, his stockinged foot caught in a frayed piece of carpet. With a howl of annoyance and fear, he fell forward, clutching blindly at Sara as he passed, knocking her off balance.

The scream came out before he could stop it.

"Ouch, He-e-elp!!"

Somehow he was on his back, his head pointed towards the dark hallway, his eyes staring up at the ceiling. He flailed out, trying to grab the banister, but only succeeded in rapping his fingers against the merciless wood. Down, down he went. Each step seemed a scratchy slope propelling him closer to disaster. The stairway seemed dark and endless.

And then it was over. He had reached the bottom at last. As his head touched a tangle of carpet, he felt Sara's head and shoulders bumping to rest against his feet. He must have dragged her down with him.

"Felix King and Sara Stanley!" thundered a woman's voice. "What in the name of Providence are you doing here?"

Rubbing his poor, bruised head, Felix looked up into three pairs of angry eyes.

Chapter Ten

Slumped on Mr. Abraham's scratchy, horsehair sofa, Sara wondered glumly how she had managed to get herself and Felix into such a scrape. Quarantine, as defined by Dr. Blair, seemed to be a fancy word for prison.

"When you put someone who has been exposed to a disease into quarantine," he was explaining to Felix, who seemed to be in a state of shock, "you isolate them, so that they cannot spread the disease to other people. Do you follow me so far?"

Felix nodded. His mouth hung open. He was breathing through his mouth because his nose was sore, Sara could tell. She could see a lump the size of a pullet's egg on the side of his head.

"By entering this house without permission, you have exposed yourselves to contagion," continued the doctor, including Sara in his reproving gaze. "You will therefore have to remain here for a period of no less than two weeks."

"Two weeks!" gasped Sara.

"Two weeks," repeated Dr. Blair firmly. "To make quite sure that no one enters or leaves Mr. Abraham's house during this time, I have arranged for Constable Jeffries to stand guard outside."

Rachel sniffed. So that explained the presence of that incompetent dolt, Abner Jeffries! How such a poor excuse for a man could be taken seriously as a constable was beyond her. She made a mental resolve to treat him with the disdain he deserved. Abner Jeffries standing guard over Rachel Lynde, indeed!

Sara glanced over at Felix, her accomplice in crime. Perhaps some rough form of justice had been meted out. They had been sentenced for their crime of trespassing, forced to spend two whole weeks in the dingy cell of a well-known woman-hater, with a policeman standing guard outside and Mrs. Lynde terrorizing them inside. If that weren't punishment, Sara didn't know what was.

Felix seemed unaware of her gaze. He had closed his eyes. One tentative finger blindly explored the tender swelling on his head.

Mrs. Lynde suddenly found her voice. Jumping to her feet, she rapped her umbrella on the floor. The dust of centuries rose in thick puffs from the carpet.

"There is absolutely no reason why I should

remain here, Doctor. I was vaccinated for the smallpox not three weeks ago, as were all sensible people at the first hint of the disease in the neighborhood. What's more, I have never had a day's illness in my life and I do not intend to start now. I think this quarantine business is downright poppycock. If you ask me, I—"

"I did *not* ask you, Mrs. Lynde," replied Dr. Blair.

There was a trace of weariness in his voice. For the first time since the word "smallpox" had been introduced, Sara had an inkling of the seriousness of the disease. She put up her hand timidly.

"Please, Dr. Blair, I have been vaccinated as well, in Montreal."

"Montreal, ha!" snorted Mrs. Lynde, before Dr. Blair could reply. "A fat lot of good that will do you!"

To the untraveled Rachel, it seemed patently clear that Prince Edward Island was the only place in the world that took medical science seriously.

"It doesn't matter where you were vaccinated, Sara," responded Dr. Blair, ignoring Rachel's foolishness. "The fact remains, you've been exposed to the disease and you can still infect others with it. You must remain here until all danger of contagion has passed."

She paused, taking stock, as it were, of the battlefield.

ຒຒ

"You must remain here until all danger of
contagion has passed."

&

"I simply wish to be left alone."

&&

"Confound you, woman!" he sputtered.
"You can go straight to H___"

"I've had my eyes opened where Sara is concerned ..."

"Very well, then," sighed Mrs. Lynde sitting down with a resigned air, "I can see we have no choice but to accept our fate. Kindly call in to see Miss Cuthbert on your way through Avonlea, Doctor, and have her pack a few things for me."

The doctor opened his mouth to protest, but Rachel, launched on her list, ignored him.

"You may tell her to put my two plain print wrappers, some aprons and some change of underclothing into my third-best valise. I wouldn't want my best one overrun with fleas." Here Rachel cast a meaningful glance at the furniture and the brown dog, which stood quietly beside its owner.

"A reasonable number of fleas is good for a dog, madam. It keeps him from brooding," snapped Mr. Abraham.

"You'll have to write out a list, Mrs. Lynde." Dr. Blair stood up to leave.

Wagging its tail, the dog approached the two children, who sat side by side on the parlor sofa. As though to reassure the poor insulted beast that he, for one, liked dogs, fleas or no fleas, Felix reached out and patted him.

"Oh, and you can take that vile dog with you when you go, Doctor," continued Rachel. "I refuse to live with a dog in the house. I'd rather take the smallpox."

"How dare you!" Mr. Abraham's eyes blazed. "You are referring to *my* dog, woman! If I have to tolerate you and your infernal tongue and these trespassing youngsters for two weeks, then the least you can do is put up with Mr. Riley."

Rachel's mouth closed with a snap. To advance in the face of open fire is not always a wise strategy. A temporary retreat seemed the safest course. She got to her feet hastily.

"I'll see you to the door, Doctor," she said.

"Thank you, Mrs. Lynde," replied Dr. Blair.

Sara thought she saw the trace of a twinkle in his tired eyes as he looked around the room. "I'm sure all you fine people will learn to get along with each other famously." With a nod towards the children, he made his departure.

Sara looked after him with a worried frown. "What about Dr. Blair?" she wondered aloud. "What would happen if he were to catch the smallpox too?"

"Where's your eyes, girl?" snapped Mr. Abraham. "Didn't you see the marks on the man's face? They don't stand out so much now, but they was dreadful bad when he was young. He and his younger brother caught the smallpox 'round the same time. Can't have been more than boys when it happened. The brother died. They say old Blair was lucky to survive. They say that's what turned him into a doctor."

Clicking his tongue for Mr. Riley to follow him, Mr. Abraham shuffled from the room.

Outside, on the front steps, Dr. Blair spoke earnestly to Rachel Lynde.

"I must ask you to keep a special eye on Felix, Mrs. Lynde. He hasn't been vaccinated—which might cause a problem."

"Don't worry, Doctor," replied Rachel grimly. "I'll keep an eye on him all right. I wouldn't trust that child as far as I could throw him."

"Constable Jeffries will contact me if you need me. But please remember, he is not here as a messenger boy. He's to prevent anyone from entering or leaving this house."

At this, Abner Jeffries, who had removed himself hastily from the front porch as soon as the door opened, waved from the yard, a wide grin on his face. He was standing on one leg, while scratching lazily behind his knee with the other foot. He looked, Rachel thought, like a brown, overweight flamingo. He seemed to grow more awkward and foolish with each passing year.

"Wipe that ridiculous grin off your face, Abner Jeffries," she barked. "And keep as far out of my way as you can. I find it hard to accept the village bumpkin as an instrument of the law."

Giving the doctor a curt nod, she marched back into the house and slammed the door.

Before leaving, Dr. Blair hung a sign on the entrance, warning that the house was under quarantine.

As he drove off down the driveway, Felicity and Cecily emerged from their hiding place in the bushes. Tears trickled down Cecily's face. She pointed at the sign.

"You see that? That means they could die, Felicity! Georgie Whitten died from the measles after they put up a sign like that. And it's all your fault. You should never have dared Sara."

"It's not my fault she was fool enough to do it!" retorted Felicity uneasily.

Taking care to stay out of Constable Jeffries's limited range of vision, they set out for home. They would have to tell their parents. Aunt Hetty and Aunt Olivia, with whom Sara lived, would have to be notified. There would be recriminations and reproaches.

Felicity's heart felt leaden within her. She wished with all her might that she had never agreed to set out in search of Jimmy Spencer.

Chapter Eleven

Horror smote Rachel Lynde's heart as she gazed around Mr. Abraham's kitchen. If a family of pigs had set up home in it for a month, the place would probably, she thought, have looked tidier.

The floor was so layered with dirt that one's feet stuck to it. The grimy, fly-spotted windows blocked out all light. A wheelbarrow, loaded to the brim with dirty dishes, slumped in one corner, its wheel missing. Books and saucepans competed for space on the counter. Some of the saucepans, she noted with a shudder, seemed to have sprouted *vegetation!* On the table stood a broken chair, piled high with old newspapers. Farm implements lay scattered everywhere. Rachel wondered whether kitchen utensils littered the barn in the same way.

With all her heart, she ached to fall upon that filth-encrusted room and scour it till it shone. Only the knowledge that she was wearing her second-best visiting suit and her new silk shirtwaist held her back.

"Mathilda Abraham would turn in her grave if she could see this!" she moaned.

She had taken several unwary paces into the

kitchen in her first flush of consternation, and now one of her shoes seemed to be permanently glued to the floor.

At the mention of his sister's name, Alexander Abraham looked at Mrs. Lynde properly for the first time. She could not but notice that his eyes were a piercing blue.

"I don't believe I quite caught your name, woman," he said.

"My name, sir, is Mrs. Thomas Lynde."

A light seemed to break over Mr. Abraham's countenance.

"Ahh," he exclaimed. "So you're that meddle-some do-gooder forever collecting money for the foreign missions. Tell me, have you managed to save all the heathens of the world yet?"

Rachel's glance was so sharp it could have sliced him clean in half.

"As far as I can see," she replied scathingly, "there are still one or two left."

"If you ask me," snorted Mr. Abraham, "there are more heathens amongst those old women gossips in Avonlea than anywhere else in the world!"

Rachel refused to rise to his bait. Sara and Felix had followed them into the kitchen, and she did not wish to lose her temper in front of them.

"I need a nice cup of tea," she decided. "Show me where you keep your teapot and I'll make it myself."

"You needn't mind," he answered, somewhat testily. "I've been in the habit of making my own tea for twenty years now."

"I daresay. But you haven't been in the habit of making mine. I wouldn't eat anything you cooked. Death by slow starvation would be better!"

Alexander Abraham shuffled over to a shadowy corner, muttering under his breath. He pulled open a cupboard door.

"Have your tea, then, woman!" he growled. "I'll have my own brand of comfort!"

Sara and Felix gazed at him, their eyes wide with wonder. In his hand he held a dusty bottle, filled with a liquid that, even a child could tell, bore no resemblance to water. He raised the bottle and jerked the cork out with his teeth.

A gasp of outrage escaped Rachel. Wrenching her shoe from the floor's sticky grasp, she marched over and grabbed the bottle from Mr. Abraham. Before he could react, she had upturned it and poured its contents down the sink.

With a loud pop, the cork flew from Mr. Abraham's lips and hit the wall.

"I'll have you know, sir," rapped Rachel, "that

I am the president of the Women's Temperance League!"

A strong smell of whiskey invaded the room. Holding her nose, Rachel splashed water from a cracked jug down the sink, hard on the heels of the liquor. "While I am in this house we will drink tea and tea only," she declared.

The children thought Mr. Abraham might burst with rage. A purplish glow suffused his face and his white hair quivered with indignation.

"Confound you, woman!" he sputtered. "You can go straight to H—"

"Halifax!" shot back Mrs. Lynde, clapping both hands over Sara's ears. These children were under her care now, and she would let no profanity touch them. "Halifax is where you'd like me to go, isn't it? Well I would love to, if I only could. But thanks to you, I cannot. So let us make the best of a bad lot, like sensible people. In keeping with that spirit, I would ask you to remember that my name is Rachel Lynde, not 'woman.'"

A look came into Mr. Abraham's face as though he were about to utter further, more shocking profanities. Rachel's hands flew to Sara's ears. But instead he turned on his heel and stalked out of the room, chewing furiously on his mustache.

Rachel heaved a sigh of relief. Unpinning her hat, she laid it gingerly on the filthy table, having first scrubbed a spot clean with her handkerchief.

"Felix King," she said, eyeing his stomach. "You look like you could use a little exercise. Go fetch some wood for the fire. And as for you..."

Here Rachel turned to Sara.

Sara's dress had been torn in her encounter with the branch. All that remained of the golden chain of buttercups was a yellow stain on the front of her pinafore. She had taken off the badly battered wreath when she entered the house, and held it now behind her back.

"You hardly look capable of making toast, but let's see you try."

As Sara looked around for the bread, Rachel leaned over and snatched the wreath from her hands. Before Sara could stop her, she had lifted the lid of the stove and jammed the wreath inside.

"What a ridiculous looking article!" she sniffed. "It looks just like something you'd find on a grave."

Sara rushed to the stove. But it was too late. Already the flames were licking at the dried flowers. She glared up at Rachel. How could she tell her those smoking daisies really *were* from a grave? They had been woven as a token of someone's love and regret.

But she might as well save her breath. For no matter how eloquently she spoke, Rachel Lynde would never understand the meaning of those flowers. That Rachel had no imagination, Sara knew. Had she not derided Sara's interest in the crimson silk? Had she not taken poor Aunt Olivia severely to task for so much as gazing at it? Sara also knew that Mrs. Lynde's lack of tact was legendary in Avonlea. How Marilla Cuthbert put up with her was a question that had baffled Sara since her arrival on the Island. Yet now Marilla's forbearance seemed even more perplexing. For not only had Mrs. Lynde no imagination and no tact, but it had become crystal-clear to Sara that she had no heart, either. The idea of living with a woman without a heart was an idea at which her mind rebelled, yet she had no choice but to accustom herself to it.

Standing there in the grimy kitchen, the bleakness of her predicament struck Sara with dreadful clarity. As if illuminating her thoughts, the wreath flared up in a last burst of flame.

It was then she remembered the unspoken promise she had made at the graveside. When she took the wreath, she had vowed to return it.

She must keep faith with that vow, or risk seeing herself, too, as heartless. But how could she return it if the fire had consumed it?

The flames flickered and died. A circle of ash remained where the wreath had been.

With a sigh, Sara replaced the lid on the stove and set to work to make toast.

Chapter Twelve

Janet King could hardly believe her ears. Felix, her darling son, threatened with smallpox! Felix, her angel, caught trespassing! Felix, her own treasure, confined to Alexander Abraham's pigsty of a house for two whole weeks! And Sara too!

Had she not reassured Hetty and Olivia King, her sisters-in-law, as they set out for their long-planned trip to Charlottetown, that Sara would be perfectly happy in Janet's care, perfectly happy and perfectly, perfectly *safe*?

She could feel the blood rushing to her head. What, in the name of Heaven, had she done to deserve such a calamity? In exasperation she scrutinized her two daughters, who had come rushing into the barn to inform her of the dreadful news.

Tears poured from Cecily's eyes. Felicity, too,

was close to tears; only pride held them back. Janet felt a familiar longing split her heart in two. On the one hand, she wished with all her might to reach out and comfort her elder daughter. On the other, she felt like shaking her till her teeth chattered. Stay calm, she told herself. Above all, *stay calm*.

Her husband, Alec King, had knelt down beside Cecily and was doing his best to staunch the flow of tears with his handkerchief.

"Now don't worry, Janet," he soothed. "He's a sturdy lad, our Felix. I doubt he runs much risk of catching the smallpox. Besides, Rachel Lynde will take care of them just fine."

Janet felt as a bull must when a red rag is flashed in front of its eyes.

"Rachel Lynde looking after my baby!" she snorted. "Why that woman couldn't raise dough, let alone a sensitive child like my Felix!"

Now this of course was not strictly true, and Janet well knew it. Rachel Lynde was known throughout the length and breadth of Avonlea as a superb housekeeper, a maker of legendary pies, pastries and breads. The only risk Felix might run in her care was the risk of overeating.

The idea that her son and niece had been caught trespassing distressed Janet more than she cared to admit. In no time at all, she knew, the local gossips would have grabbed hold of the news and would be worrying at it, like dogs over a bone. Janet would have difficulty holding her head up in public. The mere thought of such humiliation made her turn on her daughters with increased ferocity.

"As for you two," she fumed. "I can just imagine how Sara ended up in that house! No, don't give me that look of pained innocence, Felicity. I'm sure you're behind all this somehow. Now up to bed the pair of you, before I'm tempted to give you a good hiding!"

She shooed the two girls out of the barn, then turned to her husband.

"You'd better talk to Dr. Blair, Alec. Find out all the details. I'll go pack some clothes and food for Felix. The poor lamb, he'll need some comfort. Two weeks under that woman's thumb, and without his mother! Why, the unfortunate child may never be the same!"

Flourishing her handkerchief and her indignation, Janet swept out of the barn. Her husband watched her go. Then he unhooked the harness from its rack and strolled over to the stall where Queenie, the mare, waited quietly.

A quiet man, with unplumbed depths of compassion and laughter, Alec King possessed an easygoing nature, which held his emotion-tossed wife safely anchored. Janet would fret and fuss and worry herself and others half to death if she were allowed. Fortunately, Alec always stepped in before things got out of hand, his very presence serving to defuse a potentially explosive situation.

That Sara and Felix would be safe with Rachel Lynde he had no doubt. It was the other idea that was now causing a smile to crease his face: the idea of two well-known battle-axes striking sparks off each other.

In the dim stable, where ladders of light stretched down from the open window into the furthest corner of Queenie's stall, his laughter rang out suddenly. He laughed till the tears ran down his cheeks.

"Rachel Lynde and Alexander Abraham, tripping over each other for two weeks! My, my, my! There'll be weeping and gnashing of teeth before too long, I'll warrant!"

Chapter Thirteen

Alec King may have been tickled pink by her predicament, but laughter was the last thing on Mrs. Lynde's mind.

Only a few hours had elapsed since she had

been imprisoned in Alexander Abraham's house, yet already she felt as if she were going out of her mind.

The constant grumbling of *that man*, as she thought of him, preyed on her nerves. At any minute she expected him to explode with profanities. It was all she could do to keep herself from strapping pillows around the ears of the children to protect them from corruption.

The dirt, too, upset her profoundly. She could hardly wait to pounce on it and defeat it. But short of stripping down to her shift, there was no way she could attack such filth in her second-best clothes.

"Hold your horses, now," she told herself over and over. "The cat in gloves catches no mice."

And so she waited, restless with impatience, for Marilla to arrive with her dirt-fighting uniform: her plain print wrappers.

She was pacing the parlor floor when Marilla finally drove up in the buggy.

Abner Jeffries interposed himself officiously between Marilla and the house. "Mind you don't come any closer now, Miss Cuthbert," he boomed.

"Nothing personal, mind. It's just we have to watch out for them germs."

Marilla paused.

Watching breathlessly from the open window, Rachel saw her put down the third-best valise. Why, oh why, must that wretched dunderhead hold things up?

"May I ask how you suggest I give this valise to Mrs. Lynde?" asked Marilla. Her tone was measured, courteous. Rachel knew that tone well. Wrapped in the velvet of politeness it may have been, but underneath lurked a mind of burnished steel. Abner Jeffries, being obtuse, caught no flash of the steel.

He lurched forward. One of his feet always seemed, Rachel noticed, to get in the way of the other. It was as though they were constantly engaged in a tripping competition.

"Just entrust it to me, Miss Cuthbert."

Constable Jeffries bent to pick up the valise. The motion caused his bowler hat to fall from his head and he stooped, grunting slightly, to retrieve it. As he did so, a foot, one of his own, darted out and nudged its partner. With a surprised sigh, he fell over, sending the valise flying.

Unable to stomach his antics a moment longer, Rachel threw up the window.

"Abner Jeffries!" she shrieked. "I know it's hard for an empty sack to stand upright, but would you PLEASE apply yourself! That's my third-best valise, so it is. Pick it up this minute, you big lummox, and put it where I can reach it! If I don't get one of my wrappers on soon I shall die of impatience, I know I shall!"

A dreadful idea crossed her mind. She turned quickly to Marilla.

"You did bring them, didn't you?"

"I brought everything you put on the list, Rachel."

"Thank God for that. I can hardly wait to scour this house, Marilla. It's a pigsty, that's what it is, from center to circumference."

Marilla's tone remained courteous. She ached to remind Rachel that she had been warned not to go near Alexander Abraham. The words "I told you so" fairly leapt from her tongue, but she bit them back.

"A fine kettle of fish you've got yourself into, Rachel," was all she allowed herself to say.

This reproach, subtle as it was, failed to impinge on Rachel's awareness. Her tongue rattled on, having languished for hours in the unappreciative presence of mere children and *that man*.

"It's quite beyond me how I'm ever going to put up with him, Marilla. Not to speak of that vile dog of his. Why he couldn't be satisfied with a budgie, I'll never know. "

A stifled exclamation from Abner Jeffries interrupted her litany of woes. She glared out the window.

"I declare, Abner Jeffries, what in Heaven's name do you think you're doing with my wrappers?"

For Abner Jeffries had picked up a pitchfork and had speared Rachel's valise on one of its prongs. The weight of valise and pitchfork combined caught him off guard and he staggered backwards, bumping into Marilla. He would have fallen flat on his back had not Marilla steadied him.

His balance regained, the constable tottered forward again, holding on to the pitchfork for dear life. His tongue stuck out in concentration. Beads of perspiration burst on his forehead and ran down into his grimy collar. The valise waved wildly in the air. But he who persists shall overcome, and Constable Jeffries finally succeeded in lowering the suspended valise close enough to the open window for Rachel to grasp it thankfully.

"I've been like a cat on hot bricks waiting for these wrappers!" she muttered, setting the valise on the sill so she could open it. The impact caused a thick fog of dust to surge upwards and outwards. Forgetting her manners, Rachel coughed loudly, her hands busy with the case in front of her.

Seized with a mortal fear of germs, Constable Jeffries darted away from the window, tripped over the pitchfork and tumbled in a heap in the dirt. Snatching off his hat, he covered his face with it protectively.

"Mrs. Lynde. Please shut that window!" he whimpered, his voice muffled by the thick felt. "You're spreading them germs somethin' terrible!"

It was all too much for Marilla. Were she to stay a moment longer, she feared she would give them both a piece of her mind.

Without another word, she climbed back into the buggy and drove off.

Chapter Fourteen

Very late that night, two exhausted children fell into their beds. Never in their whole lives had they worked so hard, for the wrapper-clad Mrs. Lynde was a stern taskmaster. Yet as they headed to their rest, they felt a certain satisfaction in knowing that what had before been filthy now gleamed like a new pin.

"Now at least we can see the furniture," remarked Rachel as she dusted Felix's trundle bed. "And some of it appears quite respectable, I must say. There's a lot to be said for good wood. The look of good wood holds, no matter how old it gets."

She smoothed the bottom sheet and folded the blankets back for Felix to climb in.

"Mind you say your prayers, now," she continued.

Her voice seemed, to Sara's ears, to have softened just the teeniest bit.

"And while you're at it, you can thank God you didn't stumble in here without me to look after you."

Felix snuggled down under the welcoming sheets. He pulled them up so that only his eyes and nose showed.

For a moment, Rachel's hand hovered over the tangle of curly hair, then dropped to her side. Felix failed to notice. His eyes were drooping with sleep.

But Sara paid attention to such things. As someone who enjoyed telling stories, she knew the importance of detail. She found it helpful in indicating character. She wondered whether this tiny action of Rachel's offered some clue to her temperament, and if so, what it might be.

"Don't stand there gawking, child." Rachel

interrupted Sara's speculations harshly. "We've an early start ahead of us in the morning. Lord knows there's enough cleaning here to last us a month of Sundays. Off to your room with you now."

"I'm going, Mrs. Lynde. I'll just say goodnight to Felix first."

Rachel nodded and stumped heavily off to bed, her lamp casting weird shadows on the newly cleaned walls.

Felix yawned again. It was his fifteenth since they had trudged upstairs. Sara had counted every one. He opened one eye at his cousin.

"Gosh!" he sighed. "I've wore my fingers clean to the bone. When I get home, I'm gonna make you and Felicity do all my chores."

"It's not completely my fault we're here," protested Sara. "You broke that branch, remember?"

"I know. But you shouldn't have agreed to that silly old dare in the first place."

Sara placed her hand on her heart.

"I swear a solemn oath. Never, as long as I live, shall I accept a dare again. Not from Felicity, anyway."

"Amen to that," sighed Felix.

Leaning over the end of his bed, Sara blew him a kiss. Then she turned and tiptoed across the landing to her room.

It seemed to Sara that she had only just shut her eyes when a harsh cry awakened her. It was Mrs. Lynde calling up from downstairs.

"Yoo-hoo, sleepyheads!" she hollered. "I mean you, Sara Stanley and Felix King. Up you get this minute, before the sun beats you to it!"

Sara rose with a groan. Her muscles ached from the vigorous scrubbing and polishing of yesterday. But as she passed the window in her room she paused, entranced, all thought of aches and pains swept from her mind.

Over in the east a wraithlike moon was fading from the sky, while below it, ripple upon ripple of glorious, yellow-tinged crimson moved upwards in waves, heralding the sun's ascent. The fields below lay still and breathless, as though in anticipation of the new dawn, while far in the distance gleamed the sea, smooth and polished as a mirror.

Happiness surged up in Sara. A prisoner I may be, she thought gladly, but it's still a dear, lovely old world.

Slipping on her shoes, she raced downstairs to submit to her first cooking lesson from Rachel Lynde.

Chapter Fifteen

Alexander Abraham slouched deeper into his worn armchair. He had been up for hours. It was beyond him how a man was expected to get any sleep at all in his own house when unspeakably dreadful women roamed freely about, as though they owned it.

He thought longingly of his own kitchen, in which he should now, by rights, be pottering happily, burning his toast and boiling the bejeepers out of a nice fresh egg, until it was as hard and impregnable as the Rock of Gibraltar.

Banished, that's what he was. Banished from his own little kitchen. Even if she begged him to enter it now, he doubted he could bring himself to do so. Hadn't she swept all his favorite books and pieces of broken farm machinery out of there? Hadn't she thrown open all the windows, letting in God knows what kind of fearful germs—germs even more potent, he had no doubt, than the smallpox? Hadn't she lavished bucket after bucket of water upon the floor, slapping it with the scrubbing brush and complaining all the while at the top of her voice, till he thought, if he didn't drown, he'd go deaf?

Once he had been able to lay his hand on

everything he needed in that kitchen. Without so much as turning around, he could tell where every single nail and piece of tackle, every lath and every horseshoe, was to be found. Now he doubted he'd ever be able to find a blessed thing.

His stomach growled, as though in sympathy with his mood. He tried to concentrate on his book, but his mind kept returning to thoughts of burnt coffee and overcooked eggs. It was long past his usual hour for breakfast.

At his knee, Mr. Riley whimpered. Under normal circumstances he too would have been fed hours ago. Now he laid his chin on his master's knee and looked up entreatingly into his face.

"No, Mr. Riley." Mr. Abraham tried to keep his voice stern. "I don't care how much you beg, I'm not setting foot in that kitchen. I'd rather tread on the burning hobs of hell."

An aroma drifted past Mr. Abraham's nose. It was sweet and enticing and made him think of fresh bread and clover-scented honey. His mouth watered. He wrenched his mind back to his book, but it slithered off to the kitchen.

Hot on the heels of the first aroma came another. This one reminded him of the salt sea. He thought of thick slices of back bacon and the chuckling noise it makes as it slips, nice and easy, around the pan.

A groan escaped him, and he looked accusingly at Mr. Riley.

Suddenly Rachel Lynde appeared in the door. Her plain print wrapper was swathed in a huge white apron. She looked like a nurse, capable of saving someone's life.

He opened his mouth to order her out of his sitting room, out of his kitchen, but above all, out of his life. Quarantine or no quarantine, he wanted to yell, I won't abide this despotism a minute longer. And if you think I will ever, in all eternity, enter my kitchen as long as you're queening it around in there, you are desperately mistaken.

"Breakfast's ready," said Rachel Lynde. "Are you coming or not?"

He stood up quickly and followed her meekly into the kitchen. Mr. Riley trotted after him, his tongue hanging out.

Sara was so busy trying to follow Rachel's instructions on the best way to mix muffin batter that she almost missed Mr. Abraham's entrance. It was his stifled exclamation of surprise that alerted her.

Looking up from the huge mixing bowl over

which she had been laboring, she tried to imagine what was going through his mind as he stood blinking in the unexpected brightness.

The once dingy kitchen sparkled and shone like a small diamond. Newly risen sunlight streamed in through spotless windows. The floor caught the sun's greeting in its washed and waxed surface and reflected it back welcomingly. He could see his face in every one of the bottles and jars that lined the freshly scrubbed shelves. Why, he could even see his own reflection in the *backs* of the saucepans, not just the fronts, as they dangled, suspended from hooks in the ceiling.

In the center of the room, in what seemed like a halo of light, stood the table, covered with a freshly starched white cloth. Cups, saucers, plates and cutlery stood to attention around its edge. The middle was arrayed with platters piled high with oatcakes, scones and freshly baked loaves of bread. Others steamed with bacon, eggs and crisply fried sausages. Pats of fresh butter gleamed from a bowl, droplets of water glistening like pearls on gold.

A spotlight of sun seemed to hover over the platters. Mr. Abraham felt blinded. Swallowing hard, he groped his way forward and sat down in the first chair he could find. It happened to stand at the head of the table. Rachel Lynde took her place opposite him. The children pulled their chairs up at either side. Breakfast had begun.

Chapter Sixteen

At first the only sounds to be heard in the immaculate kitchen were the comforting ones of crunching and swallowing and the pouring of tea. It wasn't until chairs had been pushed back and a haze of well-being had settled over minds and stomachs alike that the trouble started.

It began, as trouble often does, pleasantly enough.

"I will say this for you, woman...I mean, Mrs. Lynde." Mr. Abraham set his knife and fork neatly together in the center of his well-polished plate. "You can certainly cook."

At this, Mrs. Lynde expanded visibly.

"And I'll say this for you, Mr. Abraham. You don't stint in your larder. There's nothing worse than a man who locks up the flour."

Mr. Abraham raised the compliment stakes.

"I'd go so far as to say you cook even better than my sister, God rest her soul."

"Mathilda Abraham was not noted for her

cooking, Mr. Abraham. For her *housekeeping* certainly. Now, when I cook breakfast, I cook a superb breakfast. I am noted for that. You might say, I am noted for my ability to do everything thoroughly..."

Somewhere in the middle of Mrs. Lynde's hymn to her own abilities, Mr. Abraham had grown distracted.

Up till now, Mr. Riley had lain quietly under the table, his presence unnoticed by Mrs. Lynde, who had been preoccupied with pouring and serving. After the meal, he had risen to his feet, laying his head on his master's knee as though to say "I have waited long enough. Now it is my turn."

Without thinking, Mr. Abraham reached over to an almost empty platter, took a piece of bacon and fed it to Mr. Riley.

"If it weren't for a plentiful supply of carbolic soap," Rachel was saying smugly, "I doubt I would have been able to do such a thorough job on this place of yours. I am noted for my partiality to carbolic soap and—Mr. Abraham! MR. ABRAHAM!"

Her voice rose suddenly to a shriek as she saw a piece of good bacon snatched from below the snowy cloth.

"Don't you *dare* feed that creature at my table!

It's got no right to be in here. It should be in the barn, where it belongs."

Mr. Abraham's eyes darted fire.

"I would remind you, madam, that this is still *my* table. My dog has every right to be here. Why should he be relegated to the barn? He's a clean dog. He keeps a civil tongue in his head."

"Which is more than you can say for yourself!" flashed Rachel. She stood up, waving her arms at Mr. Riley. "Get out of here, you filthy mongrel! You'll get no food from me, you scavenger, neither in this life nor the next!"

To Sara, Rachel's outburst seemed proof positive of her complete lack of heart. How anyone could have stood in that kitchen and denied a hungry dog a scrap of bacon, she could not imagine. Yet there stood Rachel, her face flushed, her apron askew, hurling abuse at poor, starving Mr. Riley.

"Out! Out of my kitchen, you sniveling cur!" she screamed.

Mr. Abraham jumped to his feet.

"How dare you address my dog in that tone of voice!" he roared. "Of all the shriveled-souled, cantankerous old busybodies, madam, you are definitely the worst. You can go straight to H—"

"Halifax!" interrupted Sara quickly, anxious to avoid an out-and-out brawl.

Startled, Mr. Abraham glared at Sara, who stared right back. Heartless Mrs. Lynde might well be, but that was no reason for subjecting her to improper language.

An unfamiliar gleam slowly appeared in Mr. Abraham's eye as he contemplated Sara. If she had known him better, she would have said it was the beginning of a smile.

He made no further comment, however; he merely slammed his chair hard into place and quit the table.

The rest of the day was taken up with still more cleaning. Felix was strangely quiet, but Sara put this down to fatigue and a lingering resentment over the enforced quarantine.

She was engaged in washing the parlour windows, an activity she enjoyed because it gave her time to dream, when Mr. Abraham addressed her from his chair in the corner. He had been reading there so quietly, that she had forgotten his presence.

"Felix tells me they call you 'the Story Girl,'" he said, putting down his book. Sara smiled.

"I've heard they call you 'the Woman Hater.'"

"Touché," he chuckled.

This time there was no mistaking it. It was a genuine smile. Sara almost fell off the windowsill in surprise.

"I must confess, though," he continued, nodding towards the kitchen, "if all the women in the world were as bossy as that dreadful creature, there'd be some truth to that name you just called me."

"Perhaps," said Sara, attempting to put her own feelings about Mrs. Lynde into words, "perhaps you don't like her because you don't understand her."

"I understand as much as I want to," he retorted. "She's a heartless, interfering old Nosy Parker!"

"Everyone has good qualities, though, don't they? Even Mrs. Lynde. She's an excellent housekeeper."

"My poor sister Mathilda was an excellent housekeeper, too. But let me tell you something, child. Living with excellence can be Hell on earth!" He slapped his hand to his cheek. "Oh, excuse my language!"

Sara nodded. She was beginning to like this crusty old bachelor.

He leaned forward confidingly. "I mean, she actually had the gall this noon to tell me I should take a bath. At my age! Why, in the name of all that's holy, would I want to take a bath?"

This was, indeed, a tricky question. Sara wondered whether she would navigate it successfully. He seemed to be expecting an answer.

"Perhaps because a lady, who is also a wonderful cook and housekeeper, asks you," she suggested finally.

Mr. Abraham considered. There was no doubt that Rachel Lynde, for all her faults, was an excellent cook. That breakfast this morning, for instance, had been matchless. Just thinking about it caused another smile to creep into his face.

"Because a lady asks me..." he repeated slowly. "I see. Yes. That is indeed something to consider...."

Later that afternoon, Mr. Abraham quietly disappeared to the barn. It was while he was gone that Janet King made her appearance.

Thanks to Constable Jeffries's interference, she did not get as close to the house as she would have liked, but had to content herself with dropping two heavily laden baskets into his clumsy grasp. She craned her neck around his stolid figure, hoping to catch a glimpse of her son, but Felix was nowhere in sight. Only Mrs.

Lynde was visible, in the spotless parlor window. Janet could see her inspecting the bulging baskets with a disapproving eye.

"He needs three solid meals a day," Janet called out, countering her glance. "And plenty of loving care."

"You feed that boy too well, Janet King," replied Rachel. "Give him a little time with me and I warrant he'll be a lot healthier."

Janet flushed up to her hat brim. "I'll thank you to keep your opinons to yourself about how I raise my children, Rachel Lynde," she snapped.

"If you'd kept a tighter rein on them in the first place, they wouldn't be in this mess now."

This well-aimed shaft shot home. Janet had no defense. She was forced to attack.

"You mark my words, Rachel Lynde," she cried, bristling with indignation. "If either one of those children gets sick, I shall hold you personally responsible."

In a flurry of ruffled feathers, she stormed back to her buggy, commanded Queenie to "Gee-up!" and rattled off down the lane.

Chapter Seventeen

It had been a long, trying day, and by the end of it Rachel's patience was wearing thin.

That morning, when she had asked Sara to mix the muffin batter, a decidedly sheepish expression had clouded the child's face. After a few piercing questions from Rachel, she had confessed that her experience of baking was limited to licking out the mixing bowl after her father's cook had popped the cake in the oven.

Rachel blinked in disbelief.

"You mean to stand there and tell me that a girl your age has baked neither bread nor buns?" she gasped. "Why, I rolled out my first pastry dough as a little dimpled child of four. And very good dough it was, too. I was noted for my dough, even at four."

Under her instructions, Sara had set to and made a tolerable job of the dough. Rachel had stuck her finger in it and noted its shortcomings.

"I warned your aunts when you came along that they were in for a struggle. I can see they haven't made much progress yet. Mind you, you can't make a silk purse out of a sow's ear, no matter how hard you try."

Sara had dimly resented being compared to a

sow's ear, but she gritted her teeth and perse-
vered. If she had to be confined to quarters with
Mrs. Lynde, she might as well learn something.
Besides, the idea of being able to hold her head
up as a cook possessed undeniable appeal. Why
should Felicity win all the accolades in the culi-
nary arena?

Later that day Sara had scurried around helping Mrs. Lynde cook a roast. Rachel, for her part,
had sensed that Sara was anxious to learn, but
the child got under her feet so consistently that it
was all she could do to keep from screaming.

As for Felix, the boy seemed to bungle every
chore he was given. Ask him to top and toe the
beans and he sliced off so much from each end
that there was practically no middle left. Order
him to bring in wood and he ended up dropping
most of it all over her newly washed kitchen floor.

The final straw came after she asked Sara and
Felix to set the table. Mrs. Lynde prided herself
on her ability to keep a good table. She had her
reputation to think of, where tables were concerned, and a well-kept table must *look* right, too.
Why, those children flung knives and forks on the
table for all the world as if they were playing
horseshoes!

Feeling as though her nerves were being worn

to tatters, Mrs. Lynde sighed and launched on her table-setting lecture.

"There's a right way and a wrong way of doing things, I'll have you know," she declared, sweeping the scattered cutlery up into her hands and relaying it, item by item, on the table.

"Please note, the knife should always be set with the blade facing inward. Are you watching, Sara Stanley?"

Sara nodded glumly. Why must Mrs. Lynde always accompany even the simplest of chores with a sermon?

"Make sure that the fork lies straight, in alignment with the knife," Rachel droned on. "Keep your hands from the table until your time comes to be served. No matter how ravenous you feel, you must never, ever, under any circumstances, take knife and fork in hand and commence drumming on the table with them."

This idea was so patently absurd that Sara was afraid to catch Felix's eye for fear she might burst out laughing.

Luckily, Alexander Abraham chose that moment to enter the kitchen.

Rachel blinked at him in astonishment, her mouth dropping open.

Mr. Abraham wore a clean white collar. His

once shabby black jacket had been sponged down
and brushed up. Rachel had been right about that
jacket; it wore its years well. It looked as solid
and upstanding as those splendid barns. His dan-
delion-seed hair had settled in snowy submission
atop his head. The stubble on his chin had vanished, replaced by pink, healthy skin.

He smelt faintly of soap. Not the abrasive
smell of Mrs. Lynde's favourite carbolic, but a
warm, mellow aroma. It brought to Rachel's mind
an article she had once read in the American
newspapers about a place where palm trees grew
under cloudless skies.

Despite her frayed nerves, she just could not
stop herself. She had to smile.

"Mr. Abraham," she beamed. "I knew you
would try to elevate yourself to my standards,
and I want you to know that I appreciate your
efforts."

Mr. Abraham nodded hastily in acknowl-
edgement of her compliment. All day, visions of
irresistible dishes had filled his thoughts. For
these had he filled the old tub in the barn,
brushed his clothes and attended to his hair. He
had suffered, in order to deserve the banquet he
knew Mrs. Lynde would provide. And she had
not disappointed him. His eyes locked onto the

table, which groaned with platters even more
lavishly filled than those of the morning.

Fearful lest the whole glorious sight might
fade like a dream, Mr. Abraham reached for a
chair and sat down quickly, his body rigid with
anticipation. He did not trust himself to speak.

Mrs. Lynde noted his silence and found herself
fretting. Could Mr. Abraham possibly be sulking?

Not until the last bite had been chewed and
the last drop of gravy wiped from the plate with
fragrant bread did Mr. Abraham utter a word.

"Mrs. Lynde," he pronounced, wiping his
mustache with a spotless napkin, "you are an
artist of the table."

Mrs. Lynde stiffened. Was he trying to insult
her? Had he not mentioned her name in the
same breath as the word "artist"? Rachel did not
take kindly to the notion of artists. That they
were a shiftless lot, she had no doubt. But his
tone puzzled her. It sounded kind, as though he
meant to compliment her. But if he had meant to
compliment, why had he not done so? Why
could the man not speak plainly?

All the petty trials and tribulations of the day
smoldered and caught fire in Rachel's soul. "I'll
thank you to keep artists out of this, Mr.
Abraham," she snapped. "Artists have no place

in kitchens. In that respect, they are much like
dogs. That is why, for the duration of this meal, I
have locked Mr. Riley in the outhouse."

Mr. Abraham jumped back, as though she had
taken a bite out of him. He looked puzzled and
more than a little hurt.

"So that's why he didn't come when I called,"
he muttered. Then he flung his napkin down and
pushed his chair back. The smile had gone out of
his eyes "You may be a good cook, woman," he
growled. "But you're a detestable crank in all
other respects. And I take back what I said about
you being an artist. An artist needs a soul, Mrs.
Lynde, a commodity in which you are profoundly
lacking!"

He strode off to release Mr. Riley and did not
return.

Sara sighed. For a brief moment the evening
had seemed to teeter on the verge of pleasantness.
Now all hope of good fellowship had fled. She
rose and began clearing the table.

Rachel felt like having a good cry. Instead, she
turned on Felix and slapped his elbows off the
table.

"Manners maketh man. You just remember
that, Felix King, or you'll end up a nasty old
bachelor like Alexander Abraham!"

The slow, silent evening drew at last to a close. Sara and Felix had long since crept up to bed.

On her way to her room, Mrs. Lynde paused at the base of the stairs. She could see a light shining from under the closed parlor door. Mr. Abraham must still be up.

The oil lamp she held aloft shook a little in her hand, causing the shadows to leapfrog across the ceiling. Summoning her courage, she pushed at the door, which creaked open.

Mr. Abraham held a book on his lap. He did not seem to have progressed very far with it. His gaze met Rachel's.

"At supper you called me a crank," she said. She did not know quite how she felt about this. She certainly did not feel the outrage she once might have felt was her due.

"Perhaps you find it convenient to be a crank, Mrs. Lynde," he replied. "After all, people are careful how they meddle with cranks."

"Oh yes, I'm sure you've found that out in your own experience, Mr. Abraham," she retorted. But her tart reply did not give her the satisfaction she'd expected.

"I simply wish to be left alone, woman," was all he said.

"Cheer up, Mr. Abraham. The quarantine won't last forever. And then you'll certainly be left alone for the rest of your natural life. You may then return to your wallowing in the mire and be as dirty and as comfortable as you were, before the Fates threw us all together."

Giving him the most unpleasant smile she could muster, Rachel swept up to bed.

Alexander Abraham gazed after her. Somehow the picture she had painted of his future life did not sound quite as cheering as it might have done only a few days ago.

As she lay in bed, the events of the day marched in orderly review through Rachel's mind. Much had been accomplished, yet beneath her fatigue she felt a strange dissatisfaction.

Her thoughts wandered to Green Gables. She wondered how Marilla was coping without her. She did not like to admit that Marilla was perfectly capable of coping on her own, that Marilla did not need her, that it had been a long time since anyone had needed Rachel Lynde.

Soul-searching was not an activity in which Rachel cared to indulge. After a few strained seconds, she blew out her oil lamp and adjusted herself for sleep.

Chapter Eighteen

Much later that same night, Sara awoke with a start. A sound, as of distant thunder, seemed to emanate from the wall above her bed. She sat up and fumbled with the lamp.

Although dawn had not yet broken, it could not be far away. Through the uncurtained window the night sky seemed gray and lusterless, as though, having grown weary of the struggle, it had ceded victory to day.

Again, a dull clap of thunder sounded from her wall. Sara shivered. Picking up an old patchwork quilt, she threw it around her shoulders, then padded quickly to the door. Opening it, she looked out into the corridor.

Across the landing, Felix's door stood open. A gentle snore floated out into the shadows. Sara could not help smiling. Felix had often boasted he could sleep through a thunderstorm, but she had never quite believed him.

The thunderstorm, such as it was, seemed to be coming from Mr. Abraham's room, which adjoined Sara's. From under his door poked a crooked finger of light. Sara stepped up to it and rapped lightly.

"Mr. Abraham," she whispered. "Is something the matter?"

An outraged bellow rewarded her for her pains.

"Confound it, child. Must you all sleep like the dead? I've been hammering on this wall for ages. My poor candlestick has a huge dent in it by now. Of course something's the matter! Go fetch Mrs. Lynde right away!"

By the time Sara returned with Rachel, Mr. Abraham had given up pounding and resorted to groans and mutters. Through the door his voice sounded hollow with gloom, as though he already knew the answer to his question.

"Mrs. Lynde, what are the symptoms of... smallpox?"

"Chills and flushes, pains in the limbs and back, nausea and vomiting," answered Rachel, who possessed a well-thumbed library of patent medicine almanacs. "Why do you ask?"

There was no reply.

Rachel turned pale. "I think," she said, looking at Sara gravely, "we had better instruct Abner Jeffries to send for the doctor first thing in the morning."

Dr. Blair confirmed what Rachel and Alexander already suspected.

"It is definitely smallpox," he said, after a careful examination of the patient. "A very mild form, mind you, but smallpox all the same. I'm afraid this will mean another two weeks of quarantine for everyone."

"Lord help us!" sighed Rachel. "How on earth will Marilla survive without me?"

"He's going to need a trained nurse, Mrs. Lynde. I'll do my best to find one, but it will be difficult, I have to warn you. Every single nurse in the area is run off her feet right now, because of the epidemic."

At the door, Dr. Blair turned.

"As Mr. Abraham does not require anything at the moment, Mrs. Lynde, no one must go near him. Do you understand? Not even you."

Rachel drew back her shoulders, as though to speak her mind, but she contained herself until the doctor's buggy had disappeared down the driveway. Then she let out a deep breath.

"Rachel Lynde does not take orders from anyone, even if he is a doctor. Now into the kitchen with you, Sara, and make a nice pot of tea for Mr. Abraham. Poor man, I'll bring it up myself."

"Shall I put some of your lemon cream puffs on the tray, Mrs. Lynde? I think they're his particular favorite."

Rachel hooted derisively. "Cream puffs, indeed! You don't give cream puffs to a feverish man, child! Maybe cream puffs are all the rage amongst medical circles in "gay Paree," but certainly not in these parts!"

With that, Rachel whirled upstairs to change out of her nightclothes and into her plain print wrapper. For some reason she felt lighter of heart than she had felt when going to bed that night.

For at least a week, Mr. Abraham lay tossing in his bed, muttering and unaware. Rachel Lynde tended him like a baby. He was, she found, much easier to deal with in sickness than in health. He now seemed model of meekness and gratitude.

"You shouldn't risk your life coming near me," he protested hoarsely as Rachel spoon-fed him some broth, in flagrant disregard of Dr. Blair's orders. "The doctor said he'd try to find a professional nurse."

"Nonsense," she replied. "I can't sit idly by and see a fellow creature starve to death, even if it *is* you. Now open wide."

Alexander Abraham slurped gratefully at the steaming soup. "I detest the idea of a nurse worse than the idea of death itself," he confessed.

"Don't worry your head about a nurse. I'll nurse you," answered Rachel, swirling the last of the liquid round in the bowl. "You may be a ruffian and a blackguard, and you have a vile dog. But I won't see you die for lack of care."

Mr. Abraham leaned back weakly. One of his pillows had tipped onto the floor, his head pounded and he had burnt his tongue on the soup. None of this bothered him quite so much as a nagging worry at the back of his mind. Yet for the life of him, he could not remember what that worry was.

Rachel picked up the offending pillow and pounded it viciously into shape. "In the meantime, I suggest you try and exert a little willpower. You'll get better in no time."

Mr. Abraham relaxed gratefully against the chastened pillow. Then he sat up again suddenly. He had remembered.

"What about poor Mr. Riley? You're not letting him die of starvation, are you?" he asked. That was it. He had been tormented by visions of his faithful dog, shackled and famished in the barn, now that Rachel was in sole charge of his house.

"Why, that dog is better fed than many a Christian," Rachel snapped. Her tone softened. "Now get some sleep and don't you worry none about Mr. Riley. He'll be quite safe with me."

To say Mr. Riley was safe with Rachel would

be an understatement, for Rachel did nothing by
halves. From the day his master fell ill, Rachel fed
Mr. Riley as she might have fed a starving orphan.
Only the choicest morsels were good enough for
the floppy, spotted dog who had once terrorized
her. For him she saved the plump thighs of chick-
ens, or the rich remains of a hearty beef stew,
bright with carrots and tiny pearl onions.

Sara surprised her one evening in the very act
of removing a soup bone from the soup pot and
placing it in Mr. Riley's dish.

"Don't look at me with those sad eyes, Mr.
Riley," she was murmuring as she patted his
head. "Your master's going to be just fine, I
promise you."

Mr. Riley gazed up at her adoringly and
rubbed his head against her clean apron. A fine
trail of spittle and soup wound its way across the
apron, where his head had passed, but Mrs.
Lynde seemed not to notice. When Mr. Riley
looked at Rachel with that particular expression
in his eyes, it became immediately clear to her
why Mr. Abraham felt as he did about his dog.

As for Mr. Riley, it must have seemed to him
that he had attained dog heaven, and that Mrs.
Lynde was an angel, by whose side he would
remain for all eternity. In this spirit, he followed

her devotedly around the house. But Rachel refused to admit him to the sickroom until his master had passed all danger.

One evening, as Sara relieved Rachel from her watch by the sickbed, she noticed a look of concern on her face.

"Is Mr. Abraham's fever still high?" she whispered.

"If it were any higher," answered Rachel, "this house would burst into flames. Mind you keep those compresses cool, he's as delirious as a coot."

For some time after Rachel left, the only noise in the room came from Mr. Abraham's labored breathing. Towards midnight, it seemed to ease. Opening his eyes, he gazed at Sara without seeing her.

"There you are, Mathilda," he said fondly.

"I'm Sara, Mr. Abraham," replied Sara gently.

"I want you to know I put a wreath on your grave regular, Mathilda. You were always a good sister to me and I don't intend to forget you."

So saying, he closed his eyes again and went peacefully to sleep.

Sara sat on in the quiet room, remembering the simple country graveyard and her thoughtless action on that faraway day. So it had been Mathilda's wreath she had taken, Mathilda's wreath Rachel had burned. She felt chastened, ashamed. In the flurry of recent events, she had all but forgotten the promise she had made by the tombstone.

As the night deepened and Mr. Abraham slept his first feverless sleep since the illness had taken hold, Sara did her best to figure out how she could make amends.

Chapter Nineteen

The next afternoon, Felix collapsed. He had seemed unlike his usual cheerful self for some time, but Sara had been too preoccupied to inquire into the reason.

If they had been busy before, Rachel and Sara were now run off their feet. They shared most of the chores, with Rachel looking after Mr. Abraham and Sara tending to Felix. What with keeping the sheets changed, the patients cool and comfortable and taking turns to sit by them, the days fairly flew by.

Fortunately, Felix had contracted an even milder case of smallpox than Mr. Abraham. After his first high fever passed, he spent most of the time sleeping. Only occasionally would he open his eyes and, catching sight of his cousin sitting in the rocking chair by his bed, he would beg her in a whisper to tell him a story.

Then Sara would call to mind the old stories Felix loved best. Holding his hand, she launched into gripping tales of gallant knights and fiery steeds. Often, in the midst of a chilling description of blood-soaked battle fields or midnight skirmishes, in which the ablest knight was about to meet his doom, she would glance at Felix to gauge his reaction. Looking down, she would see that he had drifted back to sleep, a smile of perfect contentment on his chubby face.

Those days of quarantine at Mr. Abraham's were indeed hardest on Rachel and Sara. Yet they proved true the old saying that adversity is the best discoverer of virtue. Mrs. Lynde could not help but notice how Sara strove to help as best she could. And Sara began to perceive that Mrs. Lynde was not quite the heartless individual she had once supposed.

Mrs. Lynde was the first to extend the olive branch.

"You know, Sara," she remarked companionably, as Sara brought her a cup of tea late one night, "I don't hold with compliments as a rule. But you've surprised me, so you have. I saw you as a little doll-girl with fluff for brains. But you're made of sterner stuff. You've been pulling your weight, and more."

Sara smiled.

"I've enjoyed helping you, Mrs. Lynde," she said truthfully. "I saw us as Sisters of Mercy, working together."

This image sounded a mite fanciful to Rachel, but she refrained from her usual snort of derision.

Sara had meant it when she said she had enjoyed working with Rachel. As time wore on, she perceived more of Mrs. Lynde's virtues and fewer of her faults.

Perhaps that was why she found Aunt Janet's outburst a week later so hard to understand.

Not a day of Felix's illness had gone by but Janet had appeared at Mr. Abraham's house, laden with treats for her son. Normally Constable Jeffries intercepted her in the driveway, took the parcels from her and prevented her from approaching the house too closely. On this particular morning however, Constable Jeffries had fallen asleep at his post. It was Marilla, dismounting from her buggy with supplies for Rachel, who discovered him snoring by the front door, his mouth wide open, his large, treacherous feet locked together in sleeping enmity under his chair, she prodded him with her umbrella.

"If you slept with your mouth shut, Constable Jeffries," she observed loudly, "you'd be less susceptible to disease."

Thus rudely awakened, Constable Jeffries closed his mouth so precipitately that he bit his tongue. With a moan of pain he clapped his hand to his mouth, attempted to rise, failed to untangle his feet speedily enough and toppled head over heels down the front steps.

Sighing, Marilla deposited her groceries by the front door and went to help him.

As she was doing so, Janet King's buggy pulled to a stop in the driveway. Constable Jeffries eyed Mrs. King with apprehension.

"Don't leave me alone with her, will you Miss Cuthbert?" he mumbled, out of the corner of his mouth. "It's all I can do to keep her from breakin' into the house."

Already Janet was marching towards the front steps, as quickly as the vast hamper she carried would allow.

"Good morning, Janet," called Marilla, handing Abner Jeffries his dented bowler. "You're in a great hurry for such a fine morning."

"It may seem fine to you, Marilla," panted Janet, "but to a mother whose sick child lies languishing for want of care, it's anything but fine, I can assure you."

In the window of the upstairs bedroom Felix's face appeared for a moment. He had heard his mother's voice. By this time, the worst of his illness had passed, and though pale, he was well on his way to recovery.

Behind him, Rachel Lynde waved a quilted wrap, which she proceeded to throw over his shoulders. Scolding him roundly for exposing himself to drafts, she led him away from the half-open window. Sara took his place, surveying the scene below with a curious eye.

"I don't think Felix lacks proper care, Janet," Marilla was saying, nettled to hear her friend's nursing skills slighted.

Janet put down the hamper and gestured dramatically towards the window. "If that child had been cared for properly, he would never have fallen ill. I hold Rachel Lynde responsible. So there!"

Unfortunately for Janet, Mrs. Lynde chose that precise moment to open the front door. She heard every word Janet uttered.

"Of all the ungrateful women in the world," she burst out, "you are the worst, Janet King. I am doing my very best for your child, and don't you forget it!"

"I saw him just now, through the window." Janet sounded on the verge of tears. "His little face seemed so pale and thin, he looked ready to meet his Maker!"

Tears always unhinged Constable Jeffries. He snuffled in sympathy. Drawing out a handkerchief the size of a tablecloth, and of questionable cleanliness, he flapped at his eyes.

Rachel, however, felt no sympathy, only outrage. "Pale and thin, my granny! It'd take more than smallpox to make that child lose his appetite!"

She stepped forward, intending to give Janet King a further piece of her mind, but Constable Jeffries had stuffed the handkerchief back in his pocket, picked up the pitchfork and laid it crosswise against the door, barring her passage.

"Now, Mrs. Lynde, remember them germs!" he gasped, his face well averted from Rachel's. "Them germs is deadly! It's my bounden duty to ask you to remain in the house, an' keep them germs in with you."

"Don't be such a pompous nincompoop, Abner Jeffries," retorted Rachel. But she was too good a nurse to spread infection wilfully. Stepping back inside, she slammed the door.

The pitchfork dropped to the ground, jabbing Abner in the toe. He howled, bent over to grasp his wounded foot, forgot he needed it to stand on and pitched forward onto the front porch.

Neither Marilla nor Janet paid him the slightest attention.

"I still hold you responsible, Rachel Lynde," screamed Janet at the closed door. "I wouldn't trust you to look after a dog I didn't like!"

Although Rachel chose to observe the rest of the scene through the parlor window, she did not deign to reply.

Frustrated, Janet kicked the hamper and turned to leave.

"I think you're being most unreasonable, Janet," chided Marilla. "Rachel is an extremely capable manager. It's a good thing for those children that she's there."

"How can you stand there so brazenly and defend her, Marilla Cuthbert? But then, I shouldn't be surprised. You know nothing about children. You can't be expected to know how a mother feels!"

Having raised Anne Shirley to mature and thoughtful adulthood, Marilla felt that she was not completely ignorant of child-rearing methods. As soon as she could control her voice, she said quietly, "If I had anything to do with the raising of two children as foolhardy as Felix and

Sara, I would certainly not boast about it, Janet. Rachel is doing her best, and once you've calmed down to the point of sanity, you will see that, and thank her for it. Good day."

With a dignified nod, Marilla dismissed Janet King and mounted her buggy.

Sara, watching from the window, wanted to applaud loudly. It did her soul good to hear Rachel so ably defended. She was beginning to understand that the public perception of Mrs. Lynde differed greatly from the woman herself. There was another side to Rachel, a side that only those who knew her well could see and appreciate.

On his last visit, Dr. Blair himself did not stint in his praise of Mrs. Lynde.

"I must say, I could not have found a better nurse than yourself, Mrs. Lynde," he enthused as he took his leave. "Thanks to you, both patients have made great strides. Felix and Sara should be able to return home by Sunday."

"I only did what one human being should do for another, that's all, Doctor," responded Rachel, doing her best to disguise her pleasure in his remarks. "Such is my duty, and I never shirk my duty."

"She's noted for that," added Sara with a smile.

Promising to return on Sunday with Felix's parents, Dr. Blair took Rachel's hand in farewell.

"Thank you, Rachel," he said. "You're a good soul, so you are."

"Good soul, my auntie!" Mrs. Lynde murmured, closing the door behind him, embarrassed by his praise.

"You *are* a good soul, Mrs. Lynde," replied Sara. "Anyone who sits up night after night to care for other people *must* be a good soul. But I've made another discovery about you. Would you like to know what it is?"

A smile brightened Rachel's tired face.

"Well, go on, out with it!"

Sara walked up to Mrs. Lynde and put her arms around her generous girth. "You've got a good heart, too. That's what I've discovered. Only you do your best to keep it a secret."

"Gracious, child, don't let Mr. Abraham hear you! He might stop being a-feard of me. And then where would I be?"

As though hearing his own name, Mr. Abraham chose that moment to bellow down the stairs.

"Does a man have to die of thirst up here before he can get a cup of tea?"

"Speak of the devil and he'll appear! I declare

to goodness there is nothing worse than the con-
valescent male. Put the kettle on, Sara, there's a
dear. I'll break out some of my lemon cream puffs.
I think we could all do with a little celebration!"

Chapter Twenty

Carrying a pile of clean white shirts, Sara
knocked on Mr. Abraham's door. It was Sunday.
The quarantine was over, and Janet and Alec
King would be arriving shortly to collect Felix
and Sara.

Mr. Abraham answered her knock promptly.
Sara noticed that he was wearing dove-gray
trousers she had never seen before and that his
shoes shone. His face, by contrast, looked somber.

"Mrs. Lynde washed all your shirts, Mr.
Abraham," she said, handing them to him. "She
says a clean white shirt is good for a man's soul.
There's enough here to last at least two weeks."

Mr. Abraham stood in his doorway, holding
the pile of shirts. He did not seem to know what
to do with them.

"Why don't you put one on," suggested Sara.

He nodded and closed the door. Although his
eyes were kind, he did not smile.

Standing rather stupidly by the closed door, Sara remembered how one night, towards the end of his convalescence, she had come quietly into Mr. Abraham's room to relieve Mrs. Lynde. She had found her asleep, worn out, in her chair by the bed. One of her hands rested on Mr. Abraham's. Looking over at the patient, Sara had seen that he was no longer asleep, only lying quietly, so as not to disturb Mrs. Lynde. She had smiled at him then, and his answering grin had lit up his face, so that she could see, in the direct blue eyes and slow smile, something of the handsome youth he must once have been.

Was it possible, she wondered, that Mr. Abraham would miss them when they were gone?

Rachel was downstairs, adjusting her hat with its damaged oranges, when she noticed Mr. Abraham appear behind her in the mirror. Outside, Dr. Blair was removing the quarantine sign, and she had just taken great pleasure in shooing Constable Jeffries off the premises.

"Why, Mr. Abraham," she beamed. "I hardly recognized you, you look so spruce. I must say, a good white shirt and collar do wonders for a man." She held out her hand. "Well, goodbye. I put up some pies for you in the larder. I suppose this house will be dirtier than ever in a month's time. Mr. Riley will have discarded whatever little polish his manners have acquired under my influence and you'll have degenerated into the sloppy, unshaven ruffian you once were. Reformation in men and dogs never goes very deep."

At the mention of his name, Mr. Riley stood up from his position by the hall mirror, where he had been contemplating Rachel devotedly. He edged forward, his tail wagging, to nudge against her skirts.

"It's not enough that you come into a man's peaceful home and turn it upside down," grumbled Mr. Abraham, glaring at his dog, who seemed to have forgotten his existence. "But you have to go and alienate his dog's affections."

"He'll grow fond of you again when I go home. Dogs are not very particular that way. All they want is bones. Budgies—now, *they* love selflessly." Never in her life had Rachel owned such a bird, but she managed to sound as though she had swallowed the book on budgies.

Try as he might, Mr. Abraham could not seem to put any heart into their usual verbal combat.

Rachel eyed him. Something, she perceived, was on *that man's* mind, and the sooner he spat it out the better. She pulled her gloves on briskly and peered through the screen door. The Kings' buggy was just turning in to the driveway.

Mr. Abraham cleared his throat and turned away. He turned back, shoved his hands in his pockets, pulled them out and examined his nails carefully.

He looked, she thought, watching him closely out of the corner of her eye, as though he were standing on hot coals.

Suddenly, Mr. Abraham stepped up to the mirror and adjusted his tie. This action seemed to endow him with courage.

"I was wondering...um..." he began.

"Wondering? Yes? What were you wondering?" Rachel turned quickly back from the door.

"Well...I was...um..."

"I know. You said 'wondering.'"

"Yes. I...um...I was wondering if you...if you...you...that is..." His voice faltered, then failed.

"For Heaven's sake, man. If I would WHAT?"

"Come and visit me? When time allows? Next week? Tomorrow?"

Rachel laughed, a rare laugh of delight. Reaching out, she grasped his hand.

"Of course I shall, Alexander. You know why? Because I can tell you need me. And it's always nice to be needed. Now that we've finally made friends, nothing could keep me away, either from you or that dreadful Mr. Riley."

With her other hand, she patted Mr. Riley, who wagged his tail nineteen to the dozen.

A huge gasp of relief escaped Mr. Abraham. He seemed restored to his old combative self.

"Thank you, Rachel." He grinned. "You're the only woman who knows how to put the fear of God into me."

Felicity was the first to jump out of the buggy to greet Sara.

"I'm dreadfully sorry, Sara," she said, hugging her cousin contritely. "I should never have dared you that way. I don't know what got into me."

"I'm glad I accepted your dare, Felicity. Otherwise I might never have made friends with Mr. Abraham." Or with Rachel Lynde, either, Sara wanted to add, but refrained, not wanting to confuse the issue.

Aunt Janet too had an apology to make. Tears of delight sprang to her eyes as she clasped her son to her heart. He did not look in the least like an invalid. He did not, for that matter, look as though he had been deprived in any way. He looked sleek and plump as a seal.

"I do believe I owe you an apology, Mrs. Lynde...Rachel," she said, offering her hand.

"That's not necessary, Janet," Rachel replied, shaking her hand firmly. "I understand how some people can go to pieces in a crisis. Not like Sara, here. She was a great help to me. I've had my eyes opened where Sara is concerned, I will say that."

Before they drove away, Sara bade a quiet farewell to Alexander Abraham.

"I shall miss our little chats," he said, as she hugged him. "Don't ask me why, but the first time I set eyes on you, you put me in mind of dear Mathilda. I've had a special fondness for you ever since. You will come and see me, won't you?"

"Yes, I will, Mr. Abraham. I will indeed."

In time to come, Sara was to keep her promise. She was also to keep a promise she had made to Mr. Abraham's sister, Mathilda.

This time the Avonlea general store was almost deserted when Sara entered. She made straight for the haberdashery counter.

"I'd like a length of yellow ribbon, please," she requested of Mr. Lawson.

"Why, certainly, Miss Stanley."

As he moved to fill her order, Sara glimpsed behind him the wink and dash of the crimson silk. From the highest shelf it seemed to signal her, in its own secret code, reminding her of its fiery presence. Deliberately, she turned her head away.

"The ribbon, Miss Stanley..."

Mr. Lawson was holding it up. In his other hand he held his long scissors.

"Is it for your own hair? Shall I cut it in hair-ribbon lengths?"

"No, thank you Mr. Lawson," she replied, her smile sunny as the ribbon. "I'll take it just as it is. It's not for my hair, you see. It's for a wreath."

ಌ   ಌ   ಌ